IN THE COMPANY OF MADNESS

IN THE COMPANY OF MADNESS

R. B. R. VERHAGEN

Published by R. B. R. Verhagen in 2020
R. B. R. Verhagen, Yarra Glen, Victoria, Australia
51 297 128 018

Title: In the Company of Madness
ISBN: 9780995384903 (paperback)

Typeset in Bembo
Set by Up & Up Media

To what base uses do we come ... Imperial Caesar, dead and
turned to clay, might stop a hole to keep the wind away.

SHAKESPEARE, *Hamlet*, V.I, 193–204

ACT ONE

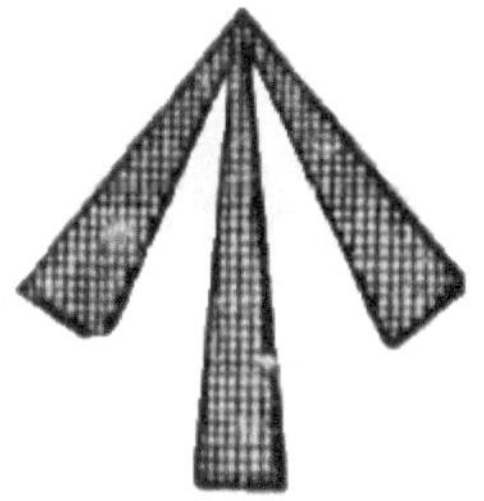

PROLOGUE

Macquarie Harbour, 1823 A.D.

There is a body on the sand beside the sodden ashes.

The estuary is silver, wrinkled only by the wind. The beach on the far side is brown, a thin hem between the shimmering river and the rising heads of trees. The trees are the colour of lead. Alexander does not know if the sun is rising or going down. He cannot see it. He is not even pretending. He does not know; however hard he tries to know. He cannot see it.

He can see the sky, which is filled with rapidly changing colours. The sky bruises. It makes the deep bush deeper and more frightening. Alexander does not know where the sun is. He does not know if it is the cold or sight of unknown country that makes him shake.

The fire is forgotten. It is now a damp soup of ashes. Alexander cannot call it a fire, because the fire is not there. It is ashes without fire. He calls it fire anyway.

The fire's gone out, Cox, he says. Cox does not answer.

Alexander looks up to the sky for the sun but it is not there. What brought me here? he asks himself. He has to ask himself, because Cox is not at hand. He does not know where Cox is.

There is a body on the sand beside the sodden ashes. It is garnished with grains of sand. He cannot call it Cox because Cox is not there. It is a body without a person. He calls it Cox anyway.

I feel like a thread, Cox. A long thread wrapped around a bobbin. The bobbin is spinning. It is spinning so hard I might fall off.

He looks at Cox, lumped in bald and grey pounds of flesh on the sand beside the ashes. Alexander does not know the hour, but he knows where Cox's head is. He turns around to look at the hollow of the dead tree.

He cannot see Cox's eyes but he can see a round white chin and gaunt white cheeks and flat white forehead. The forehead possesses a dark cut in it, filled with blood which dried black long ago. The face is white enough to form shadows in the dim hollow.

Where is the tomahawk which he crowned the boy with? Blood, viscous as pitch, had crawled over Cox's face, eyes stuck together, mouth open. It looked like tar pouring over Cox's head. Alexander remembers someone dying of that trick once, tar over the head. What a dreadful trick it is. He does not like to think of it.

You told me you could swim, you fool, Alexander speaks to the hollow tree. Cox does not answer but Alexander is used to his silence now. Run up the coast, says Cox – Alexander is chattering to himself – We won't go inland like you did with those other lags, we won't do that 'cause you don't want to. Not to worry, Alexander. We'll do as you like. I can hold my own in deep water.

Alexander looks upon the silver estuary and thinks of how Cox confessed that he could not swim. The cur had waited until the very last, until they were well away from settlement and married to the escape and pursued by soldiers and all. Only then he told him he could not swim. He had crouched at the fire and cussed at Alexander. He called him a Mary and said there was nothing to be afraid of, walking inland. Alexander had done it before. What did he have to be afraid of?

It was more merciful to kill Cox than to take him inland, although Alexander did not kill him for mercy. He killed him because he was upset. Cox had lied. How could he keep company with a liar? Cox asked him what he was afraid of. Alexander could not tell him. He would not understand. Cox did not know what he was asking for, walking east. Even the word east makes Alexander shiver like cold or the sight of foreign country. It *is* foreign country, the east, and it has taken away a part of him he cannot get back.

You done it before and lived, was the last thing Cox said.

Alexander has done it before, but did he live?

Alexander hears another voice. It is not his and it is not Cox's.

We won't walk out 'is country wiv' our lives. Least wiv' our minds.

Alexander walks towards the famished tree.

What brought me here? he asks.

He is close enough to the hollow that he can see the eyes inside it. Their look brings on a sudden illness. He is suddenly, violently ill on the sand.

On hands and knees he looks to the river and into the sky that weighs on the mountains. He decides it is evening. A faint yellow oil spreads in the west. He crawls to the edge of the water to get a better view of it.

He sees memories in the sky as a man sometimes sees in flames or clear liquid. He thinks of Ireland, far over the sea, and the gaol at Hobart, far over the mountains. Somehow both strands of his braided life have brought him to this brown beach where he will never father children, never lie with a woman unpaid, never again be drunk or merry. He would probably cut off a finger or two for an ounce of tobacco, and he means it. Of course, he would need a pipe to smoke with, and he has lost his pipe. It is a tragic loss.

Alexander looks at the river, now charcoal, its folds beckoning him in. What has he to lose by swimming across? He looks at the body of Cox, which has abandoned all its humanity. He cuts away the fleshy part of one arm. This he slips into a pocket of his jacket. He has other food, but it is rotting fast. He will only touch Cox when the pork and bread is spoiled. He has done this before.

He takes off all his clothes, holds them above his head and wades into the gelid water. Cold pinches his breath as water gropes the matted hair on his shrunken chest. It reminds him of Kelly's Basin, where he and other loggers were sent every day but Sunday to cut timber, up to their throats in dark water, bejesus. He knows he can bear cold water.

If he can bear cold water, can he bear another flogging? It is the reason he joined Thomas Cox in the first instance. Another prisoner had stolen his shirt and Alexander did not wish to be punished for missing one of his articles. What petty things he has been punished for. For the theft of half a dozen shoes he was sent to Van Diemen's Land. Is there a difference between stealing shoes and stealing lives? Alexander carries so many floggings on his back for minor offences he thinks not. He has been made a greater felon than he is. He knows there is no crime too meagre to condemn a person to life in the empire's hell. He wonders, as he drags himself through the water, if the small crimes are as bad as the large. It is a question worth asking God, if God lets him speak in the end: Was half a dozen shoes vile enough to deserve all this?

Alexander crawls into the mud of a retreated tide. The world is filled with the sound of his breathing. His blue hands fumble at the buttons of his clothes. The coarse dry wool clings to wet skin. Dressed, he pushes into curtains of reeds which rise in bushels before him.

A spangled blue liquid reaches across the bruising sky until everything is dark. The stars remind Alexander of a sailor he once knew. He escaped with him the first time. The sailor said he could navigate with the stars. Alexander sobs. He cannot read stars.

Alexander lights a feeble fire. He has failed at enough fires to know how to light a small one. He broils a piece of pork until it is black to kill whatever sickness has festered in it. It makes him ill regardless. When he wakes at daybreak he can only walk doubled over, like the hair of a hand which is blanched and curled by flame before it dissolves.

Alexander limps in the direction of mewing gulls. He can hear them, and imagines them whirling in an ocean zephyr, but like the sun the day before, he cannot find the sea. Its sound washes over everything but it is lost in the tall swaying grass.

He comes to an inlet which is studied by quiet black swans. For miles beyond he can see only bush. Alexander has felt this peculiar brand of freedom before. It is not liberty. It is a feeling like imprisonment.

It rains at night, the second night since Cox was killed, and the burnt rag does not take flame. Alexander sits under the limp hands of a fern. He can feel the impression of the piece of Cox inside his pocket. He strokes it. His mind wanders: What use is being free if a body cannot feed his self? Bejesus.

How man lived in this country before the coming of Europeans Alexander cannot tell. There is fowl on the water, but a prisoner without powder and ball may as well cut off his arms. The same is true of the game in the bush. Man is smaller than God's beasts in the bush.

They will be in the harbour looking for me. They will be scouring the coast, Alexander says to Cox. It went that way last time. That was when the sailor said we should go east. You do not know what demons are east of us here, Cox. You do not know.

Alexander looks into the rotting night sky which is darkest upon the face of a nearby mountain. He has climbed that mountain before and not come back. Now he knows what he will do.

Alexander walks to the edge of the inlet and follows its round sands back to the mouth of the river. He takes off his clothes, keeping Cox inside his pocket, and holds the dry garments in a fist in the air.

As he sweeps the water behind him with one slow arm he thinks of what will happen when they find him. The flogging will hurt for three days, then it will be over. The prison's commandant will ask what has become of the other prisoner. Drowned in the river, Alexander will say. Then he can eat proper. He will still have to face cold water six days out of seven, and the lash now and again, but at least he will not know hunger so bad; of all pains, hunger is worst.

He may never leave Macquarie Harbour, but he has tried to leave twice now and regretted both escapes. This is not to say he will not consider escape again, but he tries to tell his future self that this is folly. He knows prison is wretched and it makes a man want what he cannot have, but as he swims he tells himself, again and again, the following things:

This cold and biting water is as bad at settlement—but the fires do not die what warm me there. There is that nasty high frown on the mountain which we once climbed and I did not come back from. And there is the shape of Cox here in this left hand.

He seizes the imagination of water and mountain and flesh. He tells himself to remember them when the pig's fat cools his wounds and the pain of flogging fades and he thinks once more escape is good.

Alexander is distracted by these thoughts and drops his clothes in the water. When he scoops them into the air again he feels the bit of Cox in both palms, wrapped inside wet wool.

Yes, it is mostly Cox you should think of, he says to himself.

He is in the middle of the river when he feels the prick of another insistent thought: What if commandant does not believe you were drowned, Cox? Then I will hang. Are you better off dead, are you, Cox?

There is no answer.

Alexander doubts Cox is hungry, wherever he is. But how much can a man really enjoy death? Alexander could drown himself in this river. He knows he could. But he has come so far – to take his own life would be a waste. The suffering would be meaningless then.

Alexander crawls up the beach and spreads his lank garments on the sand. You have not been wasted, he says to Cox as he strips the body of its dry black and yellow coat and trowsers. The shoulders of the coat are stained with blood, so Alexander tears a strip of it for tinder and keeps his dripping jacket on; he will not be flogged twice for losing his articles.

He takes Cox's shirt with Cox's convict number sewn on the

breast. Cox's shoes are ruined as Alexander's are but they are dry, so he takes those too. Without clothes the body looks much decomposed by the passing of days.

If you will not be wasted, Alexander says feeling his dry trowsers, then neither will I.

The bush behind the hollow tree has shallow, sandy roots. Alexander limps into it and comes out the other side on a rocky point. It gestures into the open harbour. He takes his flint and calico and starts a fire on the rocks. When it is high and hot he casts his jacket onto it; smothered, putrid billows choke him. There is a schooner on the water, not quite on the horizon, but close enough to it. The wind pushes satin creases of smoke across the water in the direction of the boat. The sails cut in half and the booms turn. Alexander sits on the rocks and waits. Whatever has brought him to this shore, he decides that it will carry him no further. This next path will be made by his own hands.

PEARCE

Hobart-town, 3 years earlier …

Alexander Pearce has five sisters. He figures their faces like oval plates of pipeclay with dull impressions for eyes and pallid mouths. He remembers the gutter where they stood in a line, waiting to be rid of their only brother – a cobbled drain decorated with the slag of butcher's offal and beaded with puddles of brown water. The tallest stood in the middle like a cold wax candle.

He knew then, as he stepped free of the county gaol in Monaghan, their hollow faces would linger with him – it was the weird assortment of their heights and their drawn, colourless cheeks and the absence of his mother, the shortest of his family's women. The dank smell of butcher's offal ties the memory together. He remembers them this way, even now.

Alexander remembers when his youngest sister was born. He was eight or nine then. It was a terrible year, and he would rather not remember it, but he cannot avoid the vivid uninvited sight of a baby's purple head sticking out his mother's gowl which brings it all back. He sees his mam's narrow eyes steamy with tears; his father's dark, brooding face and reticent arms straight against his sides. His father was seldom home in the light those days and only returned when the sun was down. He smelled of soil and smoke and gunpowder, and sometimes all three things at once, which had the effect of green dung on the nostrils. Alexander knew what powder smelled liked at that age because Paddy O'Neil's father had a cache of it at their farm. Paddy once shoved his hand inside and pulled out a fistful of black grains which sieved between his fingers like flour. Alexander thinks if there is an age where it is a crime to know what gunpowder is, eight or nine might be it.

His father's caustic face was often, late at night, streaked with broken cakes of mud. He would check his face in a piece of glass and take care to scrub it clean. This happened more than once which made Alexander believe his father had dirtied his face on purpose.

When he learned what his father was doing, his father brought him into it. It was as though, once he knew, he could not carry on being a child anymore. Alexander wishes now his father hadn't. He might have become a different person.

He was given errands, which excited him as a boy. He had never worked before, except to watch his father's sheep. He had often wondered if he would ever be anything more than a shepherd's boy, and when his father gave him work he thought it was his famous day. His mother, Bríd, even kissed him on the forehead and called him her little man. It is something Alexander has never forgotten.

It was his job to travel from place to place collecting pieces of iron. His father stressed the importance of the errand. He told him a child would not be suspected walking from home-fire to home-fire, bothy to bothy, where smithies were hidden and strange pieces of curved iron cooked and cooled. They were given a few pieces at each place in little black bags with draw-strings pulled tight. Sometimes the women gave him oatcakes and pieces of fish in cold clay dishes, but the men were awfully serious when handing across the bags.

Those days taught Alexander the fear of the quiet country. As a little boy he had thought any place touched by sunlight a good place. Now he learned that day might be as menacing as the night.

He and Paddy looked at rooves of keef the valley over, suspicious of who lived in them. They crept through prickly rows of furze and whins on county borders; walked with pace, but did not run, through the smut of diseased cornfields. They saw fences which his father's friends had pulled down.

There were smouldering heaps of crops in places, which was queer to him because he was often hungry and he thought his father would be better to steal the food of rich protestant houses rather than burn it. Once he saw a houghed cow limp across his path and die in the ditch below the road. Its leg was tragically maimed.

He asked himself then what these pieces of metal he was collecting were used for. He had seen them strapped to long poles. And when his job was done he saw his father hold one up to inspect its straightness. His face was black with mud so that only the whites of his eyes showed. His hair was cropped close to his scalp. He had a green coat on. Alexander was frightened by his own father then.

He was not alone in the way he covered his face. There was not an inch of bare skin on the face of any man or woman when Alexander and Paddy brought in the last pike heads. Alexander thought of the limping cow and the smoking crops and believed the perpetrators kept themselves hidden by muddy faces. All the men wore their hair cut short too. It was some argument against the long wigs which judges wore, judges who threw catholics in prison. Alexander did not say a thing, thinking his squeaky voice might show his fear.

The people at the meeting lifted Alexander and Paddy into the air on their hands. Alexander wanted to be put down. They were all so happy and he could think only of the limping cow. He felt rotten. He wanted to go home to his sisters. But the friends of his father cheered and called them heroes. They carried them to the end of the meeting house where they were put down on the earthen floor.

In front of them the ground was packed into a pale mark as if pressed by many knees. Above them on the rude plaster wall was hung a wooden work-piece in the stain of its own shadow. It was made in the shape of a cross with a writhing body stuck to it, both arms spread out as if illustrating the length of a certain thing. A little wooden face was panicked and desperate, its fine wooden cheeks carved with tears. The carpenter had taken great care to show racks of ribs against a meagre belly. The whole contorted body was indivisible from the cross, however sorely it seemed the little wooden man wished to be rid of it. Pity filled Alexander's stomach. It was only wood, but he felt damaged by the sadness of the little snared person, stark black against the plaster wall.

Pray to Jesus, boys, one of the adults instructed, staring with haunting insistence at the wall. And pray to His Father what sent Him, and the good Holy Ghost.

Alexander tried to pray but he and Paddy's small voices were interrupted by a broad man with a calming tone. He said they had done the Defenders good. He crouched in front of them, obscuring Alexander's view of the tortured figure. That was what the adults called themselves – Defenders. He gave each of them a small brooch. Alexander thought his brooch was a seashell. He touched it with all his fingers and felt small ridges on it. Paddy told him it was a loaf of bread made from clay. It had on it the words liberty and death. Alexander wondered what bread had to do with liberty.

It is decades later now, and Alexander still have five sisters, if they yet live. He feels in a very deep place at the back of his chest that his mother has not passed either; he says her name often in prayer. His father is no longer alive. Ballinamuck took him away.

They have not written him. He could pay a literate person the shilling piece of a Spanish dollar to write a letter to his family, but there are better ways to spend a shilling piece. Why would he write them when he does not know if they even want to hear from him? They have probably forgotten him. But he cannot forget them.

The silence of spare moments bruises Alexander's memory, so he lingers around others in the hope that their bickering and muddled, provincial voices will break his long trails of thought. Today he stands around a soldier, sailor and a prisoner whom he knows.

What is the difference between a catholic and a protestant? The question belongs to Private Reynolds, who stands beside a short Asian sailor in the afternoon shadows of the court house.

Are you joking, are you? says Thomas Caldwell, Alexander's mate.

No. The lascar wants to know.

Alexander looks at the Asian face of the lascar, which is a name for Asian sailors. Alexander does not know his name. He sees Reynolds's face, who is a protestant, and Caldwell's, who is a catholic, and turns back on the lascar who he guesses is neither. He is only guessing he is neither, because if the lascar does not know the difference in Christians then he cannot be one. A catholic is born knowing the difference, though he may not be able to explain it. Alexander knows the difference because he was born a catholic.

A catholic puts his faith in signs. A protestant puts his faith in words.

Alexander thinks Caldwell's explanation fine and well-phrased.

Does that make a catholic who believes in words a heretic?

It may.

Reynolds looks at the lascar. He opens his mouth to explain but seems tired by the thought. Forget it, Frank, you wouldn't understand. He smiles at Caldwell and asks instead: Go on, Tommy. Ask me the difference.

What's the difference, Reynolds, between a catholic and a protestant?

The right to vote.

Caldwell is cold and does not laugh. Alexander stares long at the lascar who Reynolds calls Frank. The name of Frank does not fit him. It does not suit the black wires of his moustache or the vague glance of his inattentive eyes or the orange brown of his sun-tanned skin. Alexander cannot say what a Frank should look like, but he does not think many men of the Indies are born Frank.

He can tell Reynolds is an Englishman from his voice, and Caldwell an Irishman. It is the same way you might know a person is Dutch or French − by their look or sound. You might assume a person is catholic because they are Irish, but there are still enough Irish who are protestants, so they meet in different churches and sometimes name their babies different names to avoid the confusion. That does not help the unschooled eye, Alexander thinks, so the eye needs schooling. Alexander's whole life has been an education on the topic, come to think it through. If he closed his mouth and did not speak and did not wear anything in particular but something very plain, Alexander thinks it would be very hard to tell if he were Roman catholic or Irish or a government prisoner at all. He is only catholic because he calls a priest father, only Irish for his accent, only a prisoner for his dress – without these things, what is he? Reynolds only calls Frank a lascar because of his orange brown skin. Alexander briefly wonders what people would think if Frank opened his mouth and Irish vowels came out. Now wouldn't that confuse everything.

Alexander has known Thomas Caldwell since they were locked up in Spike Island. It is a foul spot on Cork Harbour's greasy surface, the very lowest port in Ireland, where prisoners are loaded in ships bound for distant ports, ports they do not expect to return from.

None of the prisoners at Spike were older than he and Caldwell. They took a graft to one another because they were both poor boys from Monaghan who carried seven-year sentences – judges had told them they had thieved and that they were to be transported to the far ends of the Earth for it. They are both thirty year of age, although Caldwell is taller. They must have been children together, Alexander thinks often in spare moments. Perhaps their fathers had fought side by side at Ballinamuck.

Alexander wonders if Caldwell has a family. Caldwell has not spoken of it if he does, so Alexander keeps quiet about his own sisters and the privation of his mother. The silence does not help him forget.

Reynolds's joke is not funny. Frank the lascar does not laugh because he does not know what it means. Alexander and Caldwell do not laugh because they know what it means. A protestant can jibe about the rights of a catholic because protestants have all the rights — that is the difference. But a catholic cannot jibe about it. Power has a punishing counterweight to it which never lets the small argument win.

Reynolds is not all bad. If he was a catholic he would be a lot better, but then he probably wouldn't be a soldier. Maybe he would be a prisoner.

Caldwell tells Reynolds about a very dark place where he can put his vote, and he walks away. Alexander follows him. They walk in the wide road which is yellow and pock-marked by rain. It has been made by prisoners, this road, and it shows. Alexander does not pretend to know how roads should be made, but it is the job he and Caldwell have been given, five and a half days out of seven.

When they are not sweating at the mattock building roads, under the watch of the straight, cold, eagle Lieutenant John Cuthbertson — who is a bally protestant fiend of all his inches and very likely the son of the devil, and a very pale unhandsome man to boot — they are at the Hope and Anchor which is where they go now.

Caldwell has a lot in common with Alexander, which is why Alexander follows him around. They carry a lot of sores together. But one sore which Caldwell tickles and whinges about daily is the work. It is the one thing that drives them apart.

Alexander likes the blood in his legs, pulsing in his hams and muscles, feeling like it is trying to get out. When they were on the boat, they could not go anywhere to get away from the defiling smell of vomit; his legs felt little more than bones in stockings of skin.

Caldwell cannot enlist Alexander to complain about work, so he finds others to complain with. Alexander stays quiet – as he was quiet when the old rebels called his boyhood self a hero – because he likes the work. He is told everyday he is not good at it, but he ignores those words.

He does not want to complain, because then the horrible, acrid, piss and shit journey was for nothing. If he wanted to complain, he could complain about the rotten lot of it. He could complain that his sisters had not written him and complain that his mother had not even come to see him off in Monaghan. But he doesn't. He wishes to leave Ireland behind.

But no one is helping. When Reynolds prods their catholic pride and when Caldwell dredges the old country up and when Lieutenant Cuthbertson calls them croppies, Alexander sees Ireland everywhere.

Van Diemen's Land is a much-deformed caricature of the old country – its air is not wet and heavy, instead it is clear with the smell of sap which bubbles red in the gaps of hale trees. This country is all sky, wide and broad and blue and empty, where Ireland is a narrow grey sky with not much room for the clouds to move.

There is not the glut of Ireland's green-yellow, overfed

pastures. But there is Ireland in other parts of it, the parts that the people bring with them. Voices, words, names. There is no church for catholics in Van Diemen's Land – only the protestant one. It is called St David's and the minister is called Robert Knopwood, and both remind Alexander of Ireland in ways he would rather forget. These are the parts that matter and the reason why Reynolds can jibe, but Alexander cannot.

At the Hope and Anchor Alexander drifts into the company of boorish Joseph Saunders. He cannot be missed in the pub. He is almost the only man inside dressed in black and yellow, the getup of secondary offenders. All the other prisoners are dressed blue and brown in short coats with caps and regular trowsers. Saunders is a repeat offender, so he wears chains and a chequered costume half coal and half canary yellow – but he wears the clothes like they are his own. The sleeves of his jacket are folded up to the crooks of his elbows and he wears his cap where the scruff of his neck meets his ears. He is a rare man who does not look punished even in chains.

Caldwell tells Alexander to come away but he ignores him. Caldwell tells Alexander Saunders is not a ripe fig, but then Alexander thinks none of them are ripe figs else they would not be in the situation they are in – living under curfew in a hackneyed British town on the edge of the known world building roads what turn to mud. At least Saunders is a protestant who tells a ripping good yarn. For a while Alexander can forget he is a catholic. He can forget the common hurts between him and Caldwell because he has nothing in common with Joseph Saunders.

Alexander looks at Saunders, sitting on a wonky stool in his corner with people all around him. He thinks that chains suit the Englishman's thick wilful arms which make frigid toneless noise when they illustrate his uncouth words. The people around him do not seem to care that he is uncivilised. Alexander says nothing about it. He goes unnoticed by the company, which he likes. He pretends he isn't catholic, which is a sin, but he does not care.

What makes Saunders funny, though he may not know it, is that everything he says is a lie. He says that seven years means life for every prisoner, and that the government will never let any of them be free. Since coming to the settlement Alexander has met numerous prisoners whose seven-year sentences have expired. They have built cheap skilling huts at their own expense and have been given certificates of freedom. Yes, skillings are little better than bog houses, but they are homes, and however reluctant they may be to admit, they might be the first unbroken homes these convicts have ever known.

But Saunders hates the work. It is because of the hatred of crushing rock that he whines, and because of his complaints that he must wear irons at all hours. But no matter how cumbersome the judges make his burdens, it seems the heavier he is leaden the more he wishes to spring away. He says the irons are unfairly slapped upon him, but Alexander thinks Saunders is the only one to fashion them.

The day that follows is Sunday, and in the morning, Caldwell encourages Alexander to come with him to the house of Patrick Hart. They have not been in the colony long and Alexander reads a desire in Caldwell's face to have more friends. Alexander is satisfied with his single friendship, but this makes their company lopsided. There is no catholic minister in the colony, so after their government-sanctioned attendance at the church of St David's, Caldwell takes Alexander to Hart's house for communion.

Alexander hates it as soon as he sets foot inside. There is the smell of tar in the stale air. Caldwell points to the edges of the low windows brushed black and says it is for the morning damp which comes off the bay, but the smell reminds Alexander of something horrible which he labours to forget.

Caldwell treats Patrick Hart like a prophet on account of the bald part of his head. An orange cowlick is oiled at the height of his brow, and there are some strands at his ribbed ears, but when Hart lowers his face Alexander is appalled by the view of a foxpapered skull with barely a veil of tissue to cover the bone.

There is a tortured fracture where his hair was once ripped from his head. Caldwell treats him like a prophet because he survived a pitchcapping.

It explains why the smell of the windowsills ruins Alexander's stomach as it tickles the top of his throat. This is the second thing Alexander does not like. He was a boy when men his mother knew were killed by having linen caps of boiling pitch placed upon their heads and ripped off when cool. The event has clearly made Hart a crotchety, pious prisoner.

His face is a petrified relief of severe blue eyes and gaunt whey cheeks caved by pox. He claws up his sleeve and bares a tattoo on his forearm: the faded letters *D* and *L*. This is the third thing Alexander does not like. He has seen this tattoo before, on the arms of his father's friends. He touches his old brooch inside his pocket but does not take it out.

Tommy says you been hanging about with protestants and lobsters at the pub, Hart says at last.

The only lobster Alexander knows is Private Reynolds – called lobster because of his red coat – and Caldwell was the one who introduced them. He scowls at Caldwell.

Caldwell must be thick because he smiles. Do you know Patrick here is a Defender? he says.

I thought all the Defenders were killed after the rising? Alexander asks.

Death or liberty, Hart pronounces over a breath, regarding the blue stains on his own naked forearm. The fourth thing that frustrates Alexander is that Hart does not answer his question. Instead he turns to the others and announces that he will begin to pray. Alexander does not see how this man can be their priest. Caldwell looks romantically on him because he calls himself Defender – Alexander would not care if he was the drunkest daughter of the king of the Indies – he has known Defenders and they are all scuts. Worse than scuts. Dead scuts.

Alexander wants to leave but he cannot pull himself up from his knees, the penitent position that Caldwell and the other Irish have assumed around him. He fears that God's anointed Patrick Hart might hurt him if he does. For here is the fifth thing which appals Alexander about this man: he prays for rebellion.

Let us not be fooled by the temptations of the flesh in this oppressive place but be patient while our most attendant God sends us the arms to overcome our transgressors. For you sent the ancient Hebrews into Egypt where they slaved, and they overcame the Egyptians.

He is truly a Defender. Alexander feels the redness of his cheeks reaching up to below his eyes. To think that Caldwell told a stranger he was fraternising with protestants. Reynolds is Caldwell's friend for Christ's sake. The only reason he sits around Joseph Saunders at the pub is because he tells a ripping yarn and Alice Kelley sits with him too. Alexander likes Alice Kelley. He dreams of her at night. If she was the drunkest daughter of the king of the Indies, he would not suffer a second thought. Now he must kneel in silence and listen to the jaded prayer of a rebel left behind. Alexander wonders what island he is on.

There is a sixth thing which Alexander notices as Hart calls them to open their eyes and turns to prepare a pitcher of wine for their communion: the twisted figure of crucified Christ on the daubed wall. Its hollow eyes give him little comfort. It is an old wall which pretends to be the wall which his father knelt beneath in Monaghan, where the Defenders gathered before repairing out to their ugly violence.

The memory does not carry Alexander into boyhood again as

much as it makes him feel like a cracked and bent old man, waning and wrinkled in his old unremitted and unprofitable devotions. He should not feel this way at thirty. His neck hurts for looking down, but he does not want to look up at Jesus. He imagines he is an old man who does not recall where he gathered his devotions, but they have been with him all his life so he keeps them tidy in the hope they one day find use.

At last Patrick Hart calls his followers to lift their heads and Alexander is exposed to the crinkled shape of Christ against the wall. He does not feel hungry, not even for the meanest flake of bread – he does not care if it really is the flesh of Christ.

Alexander does not talk to Caldwell all week and he does not tell him why. He cannot explain that it is not the prayer or the eucharist that has put him off. He cannot tell him he thinks Patrick Hart is firstly not a priest and secondly not a soldier, and that if he acts on one or the other much further it might damn them all as it has done lowborn Irish before. Instead he skulks warily about town and listens for Joseph Saunders in the pub, and when the boorish prisoner arrives with his varied coronet of men and women, Alexander drifts a little closer to hear their high heathen voices and shed the crippling vision of mangled Christ. It is a week after Patrick Hart's corrupted chapel service that Alexander is called a heathen himself.

Saunders and his attendant voices fill a shallow nook which rises two steps from the barroom of the Hope and Anchor. The pub is filled with the lanterned skin of potboys and scullery-maids, and the air hangs with the sour odour of day-sweat. Alexander pulls a stool beneath him, carefully arranged on the second step so that he may look at Alice Kelley's hoydenish face without Saunders knowing he is there. She has lovely hair.

Alexander lingers to stare in the absence of Alice's attention. He enjoys to go unnoticed. He thinks it is the only pious act in the world that cannot be corrupted by sin. But he is not as hidden as he thinks.

You had better go over there and sit on Alex's lap, Alice, before the poor sod goes cross-eyed.

Alexander had thought himself well-hidden but he has been caught and will now be punished by Joseph Saunders.

Go on, Alice, sit on Alex's lap. He's got a present for you. Saunders puts a hand behind Alice Kelley and shoves her towards the short steps.

Alice is drunk. She takes a knee but manages to avoid lying on the tacky floor. Is it a snake is it Alexander, your gift? she slurs. She stands up and Alexander does not know what to say. He is sitting on his stool looking up at Alice Kelley and she seems to look down on him. She turns and calls back to Saunders: What a woman truly wants is a house, Joseph. Can you build me a house, can you, Alexander?

That catholic boy couldn't raise his snake for you, and you want him to raise a hut.

The voices laugh as Saunders speaks.

Alexander *can* raise his snake. I am not a catholic, he shouts, not meaning to shout. Saunders seizes at this and stands to his feet.

Hey! Here's a heathen. What are you then?

Alexander says nothing. He turns his face to the barroom and shifts the legs of his stool under him. The seat collapses and he falls onto the floor at the base of the steps. His heart is bitten by embarrassment. He does not look up to see if Alice Kelley has joined the raucous laughter. The hand that picks him up is manacled.

Alexander is afraid of Saunders's face. It has eyes on it he cannot read. They look equal parts taunting and friendly.

You're a good time, Pearce, says Saunders with a punch that only hurts a little. Say, you don't mean that catholic nonsense do you?

Alexander shakes his head.

I thought not. So you are mates with that Private Reynolds, aren't you? I hear that by the bye.

I am, Alexander says quickly.

Good show. Saunders feels inside his black and yellow jacket. I got a piece of money here I owe the man. He withdraws a promissory note and unfolds eight creases. He snaps the note between two fingers. Alexander cannot read it.

When I get out this clobber, you know the first thing I'm going to do? Saunders asks, collecting a yard glass of amber beer from passing hands. There is no beer for Alexander. Go hunting kangaroos. You ever taken a dog out bush for roos? Jove, there's nothing better. But they only give us muskets, you see, for the natives, you see. If you miss a crack with them, you're butcher's meat. So Reynolds tells a friend who tells me he can get his hands on this old East India pistol – a real relic – cavalryman's pistol about yea big. So I says to my mate, I'll pay him for it. Well, my mate's in the lockup at present. Would you run this bill by the private? I'll stand you a pint, if you do.

Alexander looks into the nook at Alice Kelley but she is not looking at him. He takes the note from Saunders and folds it in eight.

You're not to ask how I come by it, Reynolds says to Alexander the following day. He inspects the promissory note in the sun. Alexander does not know how much it is for, but he knows they are slips of paper like purchase bills.

I do not care, says Alexander. He is looking at a clutch of sweaty, grey-coated prisoners leaning on muskets. Is it true the government gives them guns for the natives?

Aye, says Reynolds. Musket won't kill a boomer—only a hound can do that. But you need a musket to kill a black man.

What if they do not come back?

You'd best keep the musket anyway.

I mean the hunters. What if they abscond with the guns and the dogs?

Reynolds coughs up a short queer laugh. You thinking of running away, Pearce? You know the government will let any prisoner hunt kangaroo flesh if he's no second offender. It ain't like the old country, Pearce. No hanging for hunting the king's game here. But why any man would want to live in the bush is beyond me. You'd be on a native's skewer inside a week, no matter how many muskets you had. Reynolds fishes inside a pocket of his red and white coat. Saunders only owed me ten shillings, he says. He tosses Alexander two small dumps from a punched Spanish coin. Within the hour Alexander delivers the greasy handle of the pistol to Saunders. He is surprised when Saunders does not even ask for his change.

Alexander makes the mistake of going back to another of Patrick Hart's Sunday masses. Caldwell is insistent, so Alexander obliges, feeling the guilt of denouncing his faith, but all Hart rants about is how the ships what brought them to Van Diemen's Land are retired warships which means they are still fighting a war.

This is my body which is given for you, says Patrick Hart as he breaks bread. This cup which is poured out for you is the new covenant in my blood, he says as he walks around the gathering pushing a clay cup into faces. He cleans the crust of the cup with his grey sleeve. The covenant of blood, Hart repeats again with unsavoury zeal.

Alexander looks at Caldwell. The smell of tar makes him faint. He has not travelled all this way to be swallowed up by rebellion again.

What's this I hear about you getting drunk at the pub and denouncing your religion? Caldwell asks after service, crossing himself to avoid a heresy. He waves away the rag-and-bone men which approach them in the street, shaking discarded shirts and the bone stems of smoking pipes and mended bowyangs for sale.

I was not drunk.

Did you denounce God?

I do not want to talk about it. Alexander steps ahead of Caldwell and darts into a wet lane between the stonecutting works and the marine dealer where loops of corded rope and gaff irons accrue fine veils of yellow dust. Caldwell follows him and they exit together into the wide cart-track where Hobart's main business is done.

Do you ever wonder what it would be like if we was both born protestants? Caldwell asks.

I do.

Caldwell laughs. Caught you, heretic. Alexander swears. Caldwell laughs again. You know Cuthbertson is a protestant, don't you?

Of course I know Mad Jack is a protestant. He called me a croppy the other day, Alexander broods.

You don't even have short hair.

Alexander thinks of the overseer of the road-gang. He dresses in the red cloth and white fringes of an officer, faced black and bronze on the cuffs of the sleeves, lapels, and the buttoned undersides of his coattails. There is a queer brass badge on his stovepipe hat with the letters TALAVERA. Alexander is curious about it. That badge often catches the sun like it is boasting. Alexander thinks he has heard the word before but he isn't sure, and he does not ask because he does not like being called a fool.

He does not like being called a croppy either, which is what Cuthbertson called him the other day. You're speaking Irish, croppy, he said, interrupting Alexander's quiet conversation with Caldwell as they sweated on the road. It hurt Alexander that he could not insult the lieutenant in his native tongue, which he could often do with English soldiers – he bet Cuthbertson could understand him.

Cuthbertson has an unblinking screw of inhuman grey eyes which handle heavy with their stare. He speaks seldom to the prisoners, unless to correct them. When he does speak, Alexander notices his northern accent, muddied by the many travels of a military man. There is certainly a vocal effort to straighten and elongate the Irish clip on the end of each word. It is as though his silence is not intended for evil but because he despises the sound of his own voice. It may obscure his birthplace from his English subalterns, but he cannot hide it from a countryman. Alexander wonders which Irish county Cuthbertson comes from.

They tell stories about him at the Hope and Anchor. They say he was in Portugal during Napoleon's war and that he killed his commanding officer to take the rank of lieutenant. Alexander does not expect any of the prisoners know the truth, least of all Joseph Saunders who is bitter because Mad Jack put him in chains, but he does not doubt that there is murder in Cuthbertson's eyes.

Why would Cuthbertson call you a croppy if you don't have short hair? Caldwell asks again.

Alexander does not answer. He wonders how an Irish son can come to wear the King's red coat. It must have been inherited from his father. Mad Jack probably looks at Alexander in his convict clothes and thinks the same thing.

They are walking up the main street of Hobart-town past the bond store. A company of soldiers is descending the opposite way. Alexander notices the brass glint on the stovepipe of the leading man. He sees enough letters to make out TALAVERA.

Caldwell asks Alexander what he has done. Alexander asks himself. There is no mistaking the direction of Lieutenant Cuthbertson's snarling boots. Alexander does not hurry away because he has not done a thing wrong. It is probably a papers check. Caldwell stays with him.

Within a few yards Cuthbertson stops and pulls a square of paper from his pocket. He unfolds eight creases. When did you give this up, Pearce?

Alexander gawks at the promissory note he had given to Private Reynolds. He burns up his second of thought too quickly – to lie, to explain – I gave it to Reynolds yesterday, he says in a hurry. He is not simply innocent – a man can be innocent of a crime and still in the know – Alexander is oblivious.

Cuthbertson stares at Caldwell in his cold inhuman way. Alexander wonders how long he has trained with vultures to perfect the rapturous stare which makes Caldwell walk away. Two privates take Alexander's arms. This note is a forgery, Cuthbertson says.

Alexander swallows something hard and round. Caldwell is gone, so he cannot ask him to warn Saunders that the note was a fake. Cuthbertson does not speak as they march up the street.

PEARCE

Van Diemen's Land, 1820 A.D.

Alexander says their names in order. He hates the first the most: Cuthbertson. Hart. Caldwell. Saunders. God. God, he knows it is a heresy to hate, but he cannot remember the last time God has done anything but let bad things go on in his life, so he figures if he hates God for a few weeks it might stir him up to do something – anything – it would be better than this.

The more Alexander thinks of Saunders the more he suspects he knew the note was forged. The penny dropped when Cuthbertson asked Pearce if he had any knowledge of a well-worn East India pattern pistol which belonged to him. Alexander did not want to peach on Saunders, because no prisoner rats on another – that is the law – and he could not blame Reynolds for giving him the pistol, because it would look like tit for tat, so he said no. But Saunders must have known something, so he hates Saunders a little more than God.

Caldwell walked away. Even if Cuthbertson unmanned him with

his stare, he still walked away. Alexander had thought he was a friend.

Alexander hates Hart second because of his tattoo and pitchcapped head and the smell of tar in his house and his piety and his wanting rebellion and the screwed up nailed Saviour on his wall.

He hates Cuthbertson because he did not forge the purchase note, and now he is sitting on a hill overwhelmed by spears of grass which smell like wheat, watching sheep like he did when he was a boy. If there is a fate, this must be his.

He supposes it is better than being in gaol, wherefrom he was pardoned because of his inability to even read the note he was supposed to have forged. He was pardoned and given a billet to serve a free man named Scattergood.

On the day, he thought himself better off than all the others who worked the road. But he does not know how to use the musket they have given him, and if he was surrounded by 30 natives he does not think he could club them all before he himself was clubbed.

He is more afraid of natives than the bushrangers. He can talk sense into a European. Besides, he has nothing of value to steal. Where it is the shrinking fear of murder which makes him want to bolt from Scattergood's run, it is loneliness which finds him wishing a band of freebooters would come and carry him away.

The sheep disappear each day. As they deplete so does Alexander's will to remain. It is easy for Reynolds to say that no man should wish to live in the bush, but Reynolds has not been a flock's only shepherd on a hundred acres.

Alexander sends his eyes down to the broad blue back of the Derwent River and up the other side where a wide untouched wilderness retreats into the secrecy of deep seams. Beyond the gullies lies the tempting ripples of a blue mountainside.

Alexander leaves the waning sheep to their own fate. He spends more time at Fiddler's Hut, a sly grog shanty on the River Sticks, which joins the bend of the Derwent a few miles from Scattergood's run. It saves him from the heat of the day.

He had tried to build a hut on the sloping plains, but he broke every shingle he split. It was simpler, although it took longer, to strip the bark of gum trees and lay those sheets across crooked posts. The wind was strong enough to peel them away in the night, and he would have to lay them again. He did the same for the walls. After a fortnight he began to sleep beneath a tree, tired of replacing his walls and roof-sheets. He cursed Joseph Saunders and Alice Kelley and was heckled by their laughter at night – you cannot even raise a hut, they said.

At the sly grog shanty on the Sticks he sees black women come to collect tea, sugar and flour. He thinks the patron gives it to them as a form of quit-rent; so long as the women come with bags, the men do not come with clubs. The bush people Alexander lingers with are fitfully frightened of them.

By this time Alexander has given up the sheep for dead. He hopes they lead a happy existence on the wooded foothills of the mountains.

The sly grog hut is peopled each week by bushmen and convict shepherds who work sheep runs from Elizabeth-town to

Macquarie's Plains. It is from this sordid deck of cards which Alexander draws his news and takes meagre pay splitting wood. They are all sunburnt tired lonely men who bugger their own sheep because they know if they touch a native woman it will be their death. Alexander thinks he could have been a rich man with a dozen of Scattergood's sheep, if he charged each bushman a shilling per visit.

By the hot middle of December Alexander is almost paying rent at Fiddler's Hut. He has lived with four others for about a week. Their names are Davis, Churton, Letting and Atkinson. They bring firearms with them which Alexander deigns to look at.

Davis and Churton sweat in heavy kangaroo coats. They don't take them off because they say it is cold out, but Alexander has seen the butts of pistols they are hiding. Atkinson wears a grotty fur cap low on his eyes and a bright red shirt which Alexander thinks is an awful irony. He is a crude fellow whose loins itch often. There is nothing remarkable about Letting.

They pass the time drinking, and they begin some days at 11 in the morning. They tell Alexander they have absconded from the government gang and that two of their mates will be by shortly with powder. When they are drunk, they ask him if he'd like to join them in the bush, but they only ask when they are drunk so Alexander is not sure that they mean it.

About three weeks since Alexander first arrived at Scattergood's run, he is beating his washing in the river when he notices a punt drag its stern upstream. Two men share the oars. When they beach, one man hauls out a crate while the other strides up the strand. They wear kangaroo-skin cloaks and possum caps but most remarkable is the four lean dogs which move in fits around them, always holding their wet snouts to the wind.

Saunders, Alexander calls out.

Saunders's eyes are empty as always but he smiles, tearing his possum cap from his damp brow. Put your ditties away, Alexander. This isn't a brothel.

Alexander pulls his wet shirt over his head. He catches the name of the other – Tom Lawton. Blow me down, Tom, it's my mate Pearce from the start-in Hobart'in. How goes it, you old lag? Not dead yet.

I am not a lag, Alexander crows. He feels a brief whimsy at seeing a familiar face but soon he recollects that Saunders follows God on his list of hated names.

Saunders comes up the track and lays hands on Alexander's shoulders. His fingers are questionably firm and his nails bite into the ovals of Alexander's shrunken muscles. He does not know what Saunders means to do.

You look like a sheep's dag, mate. You been spending too much time with another man's mutton?

You are a turd, Saunders. Alexander says and shrugs him off. If any man likes to sard mutton 'tis you. What about that promissory note, for sakes? They put me on a billet and I ended up here. I did not know the order was fake.

Chase me, ladies, I been given the billet, Saunders mocks and walks into the hut which makes Alexander follow him. Are you as good as that, Pearce? To complain about fresh air when me and Lawton been holed up in the county gaol?

Why were you in gaol?

Because the bill was fake, you arsehole. I didn't know it was fake. Some forger give it to me.

Alexander did not know to believe him.

Any road, Mad Jack Robertson took his precious pistol off me when that rat Private Reynolds peached on me. I swear I'll be the death of him if it's the last thing I do.

Did you want the pistol for kangaroo hunting?

No, I wanted it for bushranging. No matter. We got out the county gaol anyway, and here we are—hoy! Churton!

Lawton collects three pots of clear liquor from the bar and calls Alexander to grab the rest. Saunders tosses his spirit back and begins to chant in his usual manner, although this time he is without chains.

Seven men is better than six, he says after a dozen pots. He stands with square feet and harried hair. Hot fingers of sunlight pierce the unstuck cracks between palings and give Alexander an unreachable thirst which the spirits only deepen. Saunders's eyes corral beads of perspiration. You won't be a bastard if you join us, will you Pearce? You owe me, after all, for giving us up to Mad Jack.

Alexander is too drunk to argue. He looks at Lawton and then back at Saunders and shakes his head. He charges his pot and drinks it down.

The next day Alexander, together with Saunders and the others, drive the shreds of Scattergood's flock across the Derwent. Saunders makes a spear from a long shaft of bush wood and skewers a couple of ewes with it. He spreads their innards along the ground. Wild dogs or tygers will eat the carcasses first, Saunders explains. It is the first Alexander hears of tygers. But if your employer makes the journey, he will think his flock taken by blacks and you taken with them.

They travel upriver to a marsh at Macquarie's Plains. They shear the flock at the hut of a stock-keeper named Mick McGuire, who looks more a woodwose than a freedman's servant, and sell him the scraps of wool for drinking money. Then they butcher some other sheep for meat and trade the rest to McGuire's mates for gunpowder, rum and limes.

Saunders tries to barter for more hunting dogs but McGuire tells him his dogs were a gentleman's dogs and worth 25 guineas each. He says it will take more than a ragged flock of Bengal sheep to buy them.

I'll take that little Irish girl you've got with you, the bushranger says through an ugly smile.

Saunders laughs and pinches Alexander's bottom. He is shorter than Saunders so he can only scowl up at him.

O! I would, but this one's a virgin. She would cost more than you can afford.

On their first day out from Macquarie's Plains they ascend into the scrubby hills that overlook the winding Derwent. Saunders leads them by a path that is scarcely discernible amidst the trees. His footfalls are light where Alexander's are clumsy.

Where did you come by the dogs? Alexander asks.

We stole them, Saunders shouts back. We lured them away from a farm in New Town. They're grand hunting. We won't need to go back to Hobart-town with them in tow.

We won't be able to go back if we want to, says Atkinson under his smelling cap.

They walk into a land not grasped by the brown arms of government roads. Forgotten are the masts which sway like branchless trees over the seaward horizon and forgotten with them the colours of nations. There is only one country, this corrupt likeness of Ireland.

The party rests when one of the dogs brings down a boomer. They are now in an open plain with light tree cover, high upon the shoulders of Dromedary Hill, whose humps Alexander could see from Scattergood's run. A mob of kangaroos pause in their curiosity, watching the seven men strip the skin from one of their own.

Saunders says he will thread a string of boltholes in the bush. There is a curved ridge of hills that comes up like a whip from Table Mountain above Hobart. In a few days, and with kangaroo meat, the party could cross 40 miles without ever having met a redcoat. There is water all the way, says Saunders.

Saunders twists his moustache with authority while the others drop shreds of pink, fatless flesh into their mouths.

There is money to be made with dogs, says Saunders as he

eyes the four hounds which lie tied to a tree beside him, long faces at rest upon their crossed paws. Servants of the farmers have got them. If we can snare a few more dogs we might sell them to others who want to live free.

Living in the bush they hear less of the Hobart-town news. Each week they bathe in the limpid water of the falls, tumbling over green rocks guarded by emerald ferns. Alexander dashes cold water on his soiled face. The smarting sensation reminds him that sin is like dirt. His uncle told him so. So, as a child he would look for water anywhere when a sinful thought crossed his mind. Even the pigs' water trough he would flush his face in, for their miry refuse was cleaner than sin. His skin became a field of fleshy boils from the frequent washing. He asks himself if living free in a prison colony is a sin.

Alexander lifts his head and sees Saunders standing naked on a rock, his privates bare and his scarred back the colour of porcelain in the sun. Saunders stretches up his wide hands towards the sky and declares their existence the envy of the colony. Then he grabs his limp cock and shakes it in the direction of Alexander before diving in.

They have all the meat they could desire, for there is still much kangaroo to be caught in the clear-felled and burned lowlands. Why then can Alexander not be rid of waves of returning misery each morning? He feels oppressed by the frustrations of their constant tramping.

In a fortnight Saunders brings them to the headwaters of Back River. One of his dogs has been killed by a snake, and he is adamant he will take a new one. There is a farm beyond the flat, but Davis has seen soldiers there.

You will kill us for want of another dog, Alexander argues.

Are you a molly, Pearce? Saunders asks. Molly Pearce. Pearce the Molly. Polly.

Alexander lays hands but Saunders is three feet taller than him and strong. You're an ugly sod, Saunders cackles. Alexander looks at his weedy arms, his short legs below and shrunken waist. They have all been wizened by his mother's lean servings when a child. He throws a meagre punch at Saunders who calls him a stringy piece of shit.

What are you afraid of? Don't you want to make riches?

What good are riches if we cannot spend them? Hobart will not take us back again.

In response Saunders punches him on the jaw. When Alexander gets up again he does not speak.

Lawton speaks in his place, not fearfully, but with reason on his mind: If we kill a man, they'll want to hang us.

They'll only hang us if they catch us, Saunders says.

How long can we range like this? Letting complains. Alexander looks him up and down. It has been a month, maybe a month and a half. Letting looks worn.

Kangaroo meat and damper and sleeping with dogs. I want a woman. This voice is Atkinson.

I'm living with cowards. You've got no vision, none of you.

At camp Saunders makes masks from kangaroo leather. He smears them with grease mixed with red soil and charcoal from their fires. The masks remind Alexander of the clandestine gatherings his father used to attend, years ago, when catholic farmers still dreamt of rising. Bones in the ground. The memory makes him shiver.

It is not until dusk that Saunders drags Lawton from camp in search of dogs. They are gone all night. Alexander does not sleep. He lays awake listening to the faint report of barking which is followed by gunfire. They return at dawn, haggard and without hounds. Saunders does not speak of it.

Alexander regrets following him away from Fiddler's Hut, although he does not know what else he would have done. He lies in his bedroll relieving his irritations in the darkness. He is floored by an unexpected hand which touches his face and then his mouth, slipping fingers beyond his lips.

Alexander grunts but the hand tightens and covers his face. He feels Saunders peel back the skins that lay on top of him and stretch his body behind. He is naked from the waist down. Saunders forces himself against him. Alexander does not speak of it to the others.

They come to a fording place the following day. Alexander thinks as he walks across the river that he cannot clean himself of what Saunders has done to him now. Here he retrieves a memory of a lesson uncle Adam, his da's brother, taught.

After da's death, it was uncle Adam who said sin was like dirt. It is the shape of uncle Adam in his childhood bed that the shuddering form of Saunders brings back. He had almost forgotten it. He still thinks it is better that uncle Adam came into his bed than his sisters'. But why did his uncle speak so of sin?

After his father died, uncle Adam made him call him father. Alexander thinks this is why he frets when he must address a priest. They called his uncle a pious good man at mass meetings. He was not good – only alive. He was alive and da was dead. Are the survivors always pious? They must be, and the dead always saints.

At night Alexander, with his fingers on his old brooch, turns an Irish voice to a banshee song. Saunders tells him to shut up and sing in the king's English.

Alexander turns away cold. In the passing light of the moon he reads the words on his brooch. *Liberty or death*. He takes up a needle which Lawton uses to pierce sewing holes in kangaroo hides. He withdraws a cartridge from a green sack and tears it open, resting his musket upon his lap. The open pan holds gunpowder. He pricks his forearm in a circle and then prints black letters inside. He does it backwards, as he saw on Patrick Hart's arm so many months ago. *D* and *L* for Death or Liberty. Demon's Land too, he thinks.

This night, Pearce rises from his place much abused by the feeling of being watched. In the night, beyond the ruddy remnants of their broken campfire, he sees a woman. She is dressed in a long brown robe that is very tattered and her hair is unkempt and matted like a staghound long ungroomed.

Ballinamuck, she says. Pearce grows very anxious. He has not touched the thought of that horrible word in some time. He tries to rouse the others but his throat is voiceless and stuck.

She bothers him with much urgency, telling him that the dragoons are coming and that they had better fly or else be slaughtered along with the rest. He asks her what she means, in a grating, throaty whisper. She only replies: Ballinamuck.

Then the apparition is angry. The whites of her eyes boil around black pupils. She tells him that if he does not depart the company of the present rogues, she will visit him again and carry him off. She casts firebrands in the hayrick and says she will kill them all, catholic filth. Alexander wakes to the drift of smoke.

Saunders, he calls somewhere halfway between a whisper and a shout. Do you smell smoke?

Fuck off, Polly. Saunders does not turn in his bedroll. Before the morning is done, the hot oily scent of eucalyptus catches up with them. Alexander is the first to run. Saunders and the others bolt after him.

Beyond the bald hills that sheep farmers have cleared, Alexander can see a flat plain under a coif of brown smoke. Driving numbers of kangaroos fill the grasses west of Spring Hill. Saunders's hatred turns to curses again as he sees fleet men sally out into the fields behind their frantic prey. They fling long spears and throwing clubs.

Further to the east they can see the faint glimmer of lakes and waters. Somewhere in that district Alexander knows Caldwell and the others are working.

Atkinson says they should turn themselves in. Saunders says he would sooner die. Alexander does not believe him. Letting sides with Atkinson, whining that only a few miles from where they camp the government is building a road, and that if they stay in the bush another three months they will have to range further north to be clear of capture. None of them know what lies further north.

Like paupers they fill their stomachs at a remote stock hut. It is here that a stock-keeper shows them a cutting from the newspaper in Hobart-town. Atkinson reads it out loud: a government pardon to all bushrangers who turn themselves in before the 10th of May.

Sounds famous to me, says Alexander.

Top deal until they throw us in chains. Clear out your head, Pearce, you fucking possum.

By Jingo, you know I'll be hanged before they put me back in chains, says Atkinson. But this is a government *pledge*.

I'm sick of eating gum leaves and kangaroo left over by the natives, Letting whinges. Saunders goes quiet. He does not speak all night. When Alexander wakes the next morning, he is prompted by a severe kick.

Get up, Pearce. The others are already standing around. There's a road-gang at Spring Hill. If you all wish to pack it in, let's go down and give ourselves up.

With great regret Saunders hides their muskets in the damp soil beneath a fallen tree. Alexander grips his gun and says he will turn it in to the overseer of the road-gang. 'Tis Scattergood's, he says. Bill will ask for it when I get back to Hobart-town.

Saunders makes great song and dance of turning his three kangaroo dogs loose. The creatures do not know which way to turn as they are accustomed to following a scent. At once one of the dogs passes another and darts in an unknown direction. The other two give chase and disappear into the scrub.

Ragged and weary they march east. The weather fairs and Saunders grumbles that they will lose the finest part of the year.

About a mile from the road-gang at Spring Hill they can hear the work of picks and mattocks. They can also hear the voices of soldiers. Within a few hundred yards Atkinson raises his hands.

You look like a fool, Saunders says. It looks like Pearce is bailing you up.

Alexander regards the musket in his hands.

They will shoot me if they see this in my hands.

Is it loaded? Churton asks.

I cannot remember.

Alexander looks ahead at fur-coated constables with Brown Bess muskets in their arms and redcoats around them.

Toss it in the grass, Atkinson says with a shake.

It is too late. Alexander watches Lawton and Letting raise their hands. A soldier stands ahead at the tail of a thread of convict labourers. Beside him is a stiff man in a polished black shako with tall boots and decorations on his coat. The officer shouts at them in a reluctant Irish accent. Pearce raises his arms. He does not cast the gun away. Instead he holds it above his head as though wading across water.

The private lifts his musket to a shoulder. Atkinson is out

front. He gropes for the paper in his pocket. Then the officer draws the short curve of a pistol from his jacket. As Atkinson fishes free the pardon, the musket lets off a crack into the air. Saunders and the others scamper. Atkinson remains in the road, shaking the paper. Then Alexander hears a second shot, sees the smoke fume in the mouth of the officer's pistol. The paper in Atkinson's hand is shredded in pink mist. Atkinson clutches the spraying stump of his wrist in agony. He falls to the ground wailing.

CONOLLY

Cove of Cork, Ireland, July 1820 A.D.

Do you know how many altar boys dream of this, being a priest on a ship full of sinful women? You could not invent this, you could not.

Phillip looks at John Terry and laughs. Did you leave your vow of chastity down there in Cove, did you John? He stretches out his arm towards the dock below the merchant ship *Janus*, where houses mount the coastal hillside.

Terry is too distracted to answer. He peers down the deck where the press of prisoner women are being addressed by the ship's surgeon.

I wonder if the good surgeon rubs his lips together like you are now, John.

I can scarcely fathom that we have been selected to be the first catholic priests in the colony of New South Wales, John goes on with no regard for Phillip's jibe.

You're exaggerating again, John. We volunteered. They

didn't pick us from a great crowd.

Phillip looks again at the harbour-town of Cove where not a single soul can be found who knows him or wishes to bid him goodbye – he knows why he volunteered. He looks at John, who he has known since college days, and wonders if he volunteered because the government was sending a shipload of women to New Holland. But then, no catholic priest of sound mind would volunteer to cross the world in the hope of lying with a vagrant.

What do you think 'tis like? John's question snares Phillip in a string of a thought.

Lying with a vagrant? Phillip's plaintive expression draws an addition to the question.

New South Wales—what do you think 'tis like?

Phillip brings to mind the confessional box where he sat in dark shelter and listened to parishioners who admitted sins in connexion with the grief of losing loved ones who were transported.

Some committed adultery because their husband or wife had been shipped away. Their excuses invariably hired that mercenary: the moment of weakness. Phillip wondered if these adulteries and weak hours were taken in one moment or one moment four days a week. He does not doubt the good nature of human beings, but then he cannot fool himself when he hears the same voice say, Bless me father, for I have sinned. How often was he tempted to reply, Again?

Some voices are not easy to forget. Moreover, they were

normally driven to confess when they received letters from their begotten spouses moaning about the horror of New South Wales. These events firmed up Phillip's natural cynicism.

Nothing quite pricks the conscience like bleating pity, thinks Phillip. It is towards these echoes of pain and suffering, far over the sea, that Phillip's mind tiptoes.

Slavery in an unforgivable land, that was New South Wales described to him in the confessional box by those adulterers whose first loves were gone. And yet he had heard from others that the country possessed an allure Ireland had long since lost: clean air and land not yet spoiled by the abuse of landlords. The woeful people told him that crops were turned away by the earth but the hopeful told him that winters were fair.

He can discard the half-truths with the wholes. Who knows what a country is like until it can be judged with one's own eyes? Only one claim about the colony matters to Phillip: Governor Lachlan Macquarie has determined that the catholics in his care require ministers of their own faith. It is more than can be said of Britain's government, who cannot wait to be rid of its catholics.

It is a chance to forget Ireland's woes, to leave generations of segregated pain on the wharf at Cork Harbour and turn the page anew. This, and the mortal departure of all his family, make up the entire reason Phillip volunteered. He has no living relative to mourn him. He is married to the church. For the first time in a long time he feels ennobled.

There are droves of catholic convicts in the colonies of New

South Wales and its sister island Van Diemen's Land, crying out for a confessor who will hear their sins. Phillip Conolly will be a light where there is none.

New South Wales—what do you think 'tis like? John asks again.

Phillip rouses from his trance. I suppose 'tis like South Wales, except, newer.

Be honest now, you, Phillip. Have you ever been to Wales?

Not in my life. Phillip jerks out his pipe. The dirty waft of burnt bread from somewhere in the town has whetted his tongue to smoke.

Phillip's last memory of Ireland will be the lonely naval bell. Its sonorous peal rings out across the dark water, giving Phillip a sound to accompany the smell of smoke. It is this smell which transports him to his crib where his mother fed him charcoal as a child to still his unwell stomach. There are other smells – fish flesh and tar and sodden hay, the fecund sulphur of the sea. But nothing quite takes him back to Monaghan like smoke.

The pair of reverends stand against the rail and watch Ireland disappear behind them. They remain this way for hours, guarding their chests from the wind of the cove with long woollen coats which they wear over their cassocks. Phillip rehearses his sermon about saint Virgil. He grooms it for Sunday mass tomorrow. It will be his first sermon on water.

It isn't a boast if I say that Jesus only preached to fishermen on a boat while I got a hundred women? Phillip scribbles in the margins of his sermon sheets.

Competing with the good Lord, are we now? Tell me, why are you writing there in Irish? John nods at Phillip's papers.

We were schooled in Latin, John—made to preach in English for years after. It has often stirred a wonder in me of what has been lost in the killing of celtic language, dissolving little by little, a fallen scrap filched away by teeth of foxes.

You're wasted as a priest. You should be a poet.

I wonder if the Irish women on-board this ship will be more willing to heed preachments in their own tongue.

They quickly turn from speaking Irish to English when the captain strides into their company.

Reverends. This must be something of a moment for both of you, says the man introduced as Captain Mowat. He stretches out white hands and shakes each priest's palms emphatically. His short face is studded with small grey eyes like grapeshot in a dry wall. I hear you are to be the first ministers of the popish religion in New South Wales.

It is something, Phillip cannot help but say. He exchanges a brief look with John. He despises the word popish. It is something of a veiled insult for us followers of the pope, he thinks of saying but doesn't. Protestant anglicans do not call their religion *kingish*.

Phillip's opinion of Mowat is rescued when he explains that he has requisitioned 26 gallons of rum for medicinal purposes, but that if the women are well they may reserve some for refreshment on Christmas day. Phillip shines on the mention of booze.

Shall we take a tour of the prisoners? Mowat asks.

Phillip suspects he means their quarters, but he does not correct the captain. They follow Mowat away from the quarter deck. Beneath the fore boom the captain reaches for a hatch which he opens for the priests.

Croppies first, Mowat invites with innocence.

The comment gives Phillip pause. John does not meet his glance so he retreats from the sea wind quickly, taking care not to slip.

Did he call us croppies? Phillip whispers up to John who climbs down above him. John grumbles but Phillip cannot make out the words.

The 'tween-deck is bilious with salt. At the base of the ladder Mowat points to a wainscot of wooden boards which separates the sailors' beds from the prison cells. Phillip and John are told they will sleep with the sailors. John sniggers but Phillip is occupied by the frailty of the wainscot. If they were on a ship full of convicted men, he would consider it a risk to his life that such an insubstantial partition separates a hundred felons from where they lay at night.

Mowat leads them to the sick bay at the narrow stern of the convict quarters. Phillip's flat hair is only an inch from the supporting beams of the main deck, and beneath him he can hear murmuring bilge water lick the iron grates. At either hand are built rooms of iron bars. Mowat calls these the prison messes.

Phillip looks ahead where four capped women are huddled in the middle of the deck. Mowat shouts at them. Hoy! Did the surgeon not tell you to remain in your cells until the ship is out to sea? He is caught on the last word by the figure of a man in their midst. James! he corrects himself, pushing the women aside with disregard and taking the short man by his shoulders.

Phillip looks into the open cells and is disturbed by the sight of eyes in the gloom.

Conolly. Terry. Phillip rouses to the voice of the captain. This is James Creagh of the royal navy. He is our surgeon and superintendent of prisoners.

Creagh shakes his jowls with a nod at both priests.

These are the hopes of the colony's catholics, James. Phillip is now sensitive to any notes of derision in the captain's voice, and he scores them everywhere.

The four women are walking away but a couple of them turn their heads at the mention of religion. Phillip is only guessing that this is the case, but he looks at them and they return his profound stare. It is either fright or curiosity or the admixture of both in their eyes. He believes in the deepness of that connexion. He wishes it were Sunday.

Creagh's eyes sit lazily in his face. He doesn't smile.

Are you married, James? Phillip asks.

The surgeon's loose lips assume the arch of a grin. Regrettably, he sniffs.

Mowat laughs. Phillip does not think it the pinnacle of humour.

All of you, in the mess! Mowat shouts. The four women linger outside their cell. Phillip collects the trill of Irish voices in some of their murmurings. The same eyes which had handled him before now relax on him coyly. One of the Irish whisperers has removed her dormeuse cap.

Her unkempt black hair struggles down to her shoulders. Her face is afflicted with red marks like blackcurrants in white dough. Her eyes keep the verdant green of Ireland – unlike coloured glass they appear more brilliant in the dim cavern. Her eyes alone apologise for the roughness in her features; her chin is round, her rashy cheeks dimpled, but her green eyes are beautiful. Yet, Phillip cannot ignore their sadness.

Can you tell which of the women are croppies? Mowat asks upon his return from the women's cell. There is no shame in his eyes. When neither priest replies Mowat harps again: Catholic, can you tell which of the women are catholic?

Neither Phillip nor John give an answer that pleases the captain, preferring to dress their frustration with jokes about celibacy and poor eyesight. Phillip cannot tell if the captain is a tyrant on purpose or simply an imbecile with hard skin. He takes them back to the bow-end of the 'tween-deck where he explains that Creagh will arrange some of the women to see to their laundry. He says Creagh keeps the keys to the prison cells and that he will lock them at nightfall. He stresses the importance of evening curfew, but allows the priests to move freely until then.

Once he is gone, Phillip looks back past the wainscot wall to the hard prison cells. In the captain's absence the women repair from their cells in threes and fours. Some smile with yellow teeth and share private jokes. Others retain a tortured silence. Phillip cannot tell the religion of any of the women to look at them. They are all equally as wretched and condemned all the same. He wonders if he has really left Ireland behind.

Early the following morning Phillip rises with his sermon sheets. He brushes his black cassock and thinks, with each stroke of the coarse brush, about his instruction at the seminary. Not even archangels have the power of a priest, said the church fathers. Not even an army of all the saints in heaven could match the godly power of a priest to bind and loose his parishioners from sin, to condemn or save them from their awful eternity. Thinking of this mantle Phillip climbs the ladder to the main deck where the prisoners are being mustered by the surgeon Creagh. Mowat and his officers stand beside Creagh on the waxy deck. There are clouds of white frosty air in Creagh's face.

What's he reading? John asks Phillip in a low voice.

A prayer book. Phillip is surprised.

Phillip and John join Mowat and his officers at the head of the convict mass. Creagh does not let up, but their arrival invites a queer side-glance.

Shall I pray with the Roman catholic women elsewhere? Phillip is fleeter with his words than Mowat.

The captain shakes his head. The surgeon is reading the catechism to all prisoners, reverend, he says.

Even to the catholics? the voice is John's.

Aye. It is the request of the navy board that the prisoners not be separated, for the sake of their behaviour.

For the sake of their salvation I ask that you give me the Roman catholic women to preach to, Phillip says all in a whisper but unable to smooth the aggravation from his hoarse voice. He perceives a smirk on Mowat's terrier face and understands his error.

One day at sea and already the Reverend Mister Conolly wants *all* the catholic women, Mowat says to his officers. Have some restraint, won't you Conolly? Your duties will not start until we reach New South Wales. You can look forward to good works then.

Creagh trudges through an anglican hymn with the minimum pass rate of doleful voices from his captive congregation. Phillip cannot hear any Irish voices. Phillip and John's beating steps must be legible to the bored women as the pair hurry away to the front of the ship to smoke, so Phillip hopes.

When Creagh disbands the hundred women Phillip drags John away from the quarter deck. They walk amidst the prisoners to wise up to their look and manner, although many of the women turn away from them. But there is a group of four women who do not turn away. One of them has green eyes and oily black hair.

You are the catholic priests then, she says in a voice that holds confidence her companions seem to lack. Are you here to make sure we arrive clean enough in the colonies, are you?

I am a prisoner like you, Phillip says.

Bull shit, says the woman. John nearly spits out laughter. Phillip fights to flatten a smile. You are not prisoner. Look at your clothes. I do not see a right broad arrow on them, any stitch.

Phillip mocks her by pretending to inspect the sweeping sleeve of his cassock. There is no sharp broad arrow, the symbol of government property, as there is on the women's dresses.

I am catholic, am I not? We're all fettered. 'Tis a hope that you and I might break free of our fetters in the new land.

You pretend you are not a priest but you wear the black and all. It is a man under it. Is it? She reaches out and touches Phillip's chest with the flats of her hands. He trembles. It must be a quake she can feel because her cracked lips part in a wicked smile. No, not a man, she says and the women around her laugh.

John now chuckles. Phillip would be humoured if he could not feel the discomfort between his legs and the hot colour of his cheeks. He is 33 year old, the age Jesus was crucified, and he quakes at a woman's touch. A priest for his pound of flesh but not a man.

Someone calls the name Johanna from the far end of the deck which saves Phillip from further embarrassment. The prisoner with green eyes heeds the call and begins to walk away.

My name is Johanna Lynch. The women would like you to visit them. They feel that you look at them with eyes of judgement. Perhaps you would like to change that. She parts with a flash of her brilliant eyes and Phillip can feel the thick assault of sea wind again.

In the evening James Creagh visits Phillip and John in the sailors' quarter. He introduces the two women who will wash their linens. Phillip recognises them as companions of Johanna Lynch. Their names are Ellen Molloy and Isabella Irving.

Isabella carries a cold and distant nature, but Ellen is a Dubliner so Phillip gives her his bedclothes. John does not remain in their company, so Isabella strips his hammock in quiet. But to Ellen, Phillip tells of his studies at the college near Dublin. Her experience is not the same – she tries to pick the pleasant moments out of bitter memories. Phillip is disappointed with the little he learns about Johanna Lynch, but Ellen tells him there is another women with them, an Englishwoman named Sophia Nightingale.

She has a daughter, does Sophia. Ellen's words are leaden with regret. Mary Ann. The girl is only four month old.

Why did they allow a child on-board? Phillip asks.

Because she is a criminal. Do you not know the criminal stain is passed onto children?

Phillip continues in Irish. How can I preach to the catholic women without the officers knowing?

Why are you asking a prisoner? Ellen retorts. Ask a blind woman where the sun sets, bejesus. But if you want the counsel of a poor girl, forget your prayers unless there is some word that will stop the advances of the crew.

Phillip arches his brows.

They came into the cells last night, reverend. You might be a virgin but even you know what that means. They'll make

Nightingales of us all by the time we reach New South Wales. If we weren't damned when we stepped onto this bally vessel, we will be damned to step off it.

Phillip cannot sleep in the night. It is not the abuse of the sea which wakes him. He usually sleeps light, but before now he had not made the connexion with the midnight voices of sailors nearby his bed and the situation of the women. Now he feels he knows why they whisper and where they go. He cannot forget the brilliance of Johanna's eyes and frets that a rough man would trespass upon it.

Phillip stands from his bed and makes up a tea-kettle on the small table. He sits with quiet hands fanned against the flames. By the feeble luminance of his fire he can see ape silhouettes passing in the depth of the deck. He hears muffled chuckles and follows the carry of low voices and the drag of slothful feet until the sounds of the sea overcome them. He does not have the stones to follow them. He wonders what use he is.

Every night that follows is worse than the night before. Phillip hears churlish throats laughing in the darkness, their clumsy feet scraping the deck boards as they tramp. Each night their callousness burgeons. Phillip feels hobbled by the captain's ignorance, who dismisses him as soon as he mentions it. He wonders if it is ignorance or the complicity of full knowledge that turns him away.

Ellen Molloy tells Phillip that the last sailors up ensure the cells of particular women are left open so that they can enjoy free passage through the night. She says not all the women oppose the men's advances.

Phillip recollects with bitterness his and John's first jokes about breaking holy orders on the day of their departure. That the sailors would commit flesh crimes in the full knowledge of the captain is mortal, but that the women do not refuse them casts Phillip into despair.

We ought to preach to them, he says to John. We can preach in the messes. If Mowat ignores the coming and going of the sailors at night—

Stay out of it, Phillip. John's moaning turns Phillip cold. This voyage is not our commission. We are not to begin preaching until New South Wales.

Did Jesus say he was not to begin preaching until he reached Jerusalem?

I know you are 33—felicitations, heartily—but you are not Jesus and Van Diemen's Land is not Jerusalem. John sounds fatigued by the journey. If the women desire to lay with the men, what power have you—have *we*—to stop it?

Phillip is not converted. In the morning he gathers Ellen Molloy and Johanna Lynch to him. Ellen is more abiding while Johanna stalks around with a smug countenance whose cover Phillip cannot easily open. Her vibrant green eyes unsettle him.

He asks them to invite the Roman catholic women to hear him speak. They must come willingly. Ellen agrees to bring them into her cell where Phillip will give his secret sermons.

As Phillip fans through his bible he thinks about how poorly it might go if he preaches out of the book of Leviticus: lest the land fall to whoredom, and the land become full of wickedness ... He remembers how he trembled when Johanna touched him. He does not think the fire and brimstone sermon about indecency in the mouth of a virgin will inspire existential change. So, he picks the story of the woman caught in the act of adultery.

Yea, a softer choice, yea, he says to himself. When the women are gathered in Johanna and Ellen's cell Phillip pronounces – in his native tongue – how the law of Moses called for the adulterer to be stoned for lying with a married man.

But it were Jesus that said, Whoever is without sin let him cast the first stone.

Phillip does not finish the story before Johanna Lynch cries out from the rearward: Show us your stones, then, reverend, she says and pulls up the grey pleats of her curdled milk dress. Phillip cannot remember the last time he saw a woman's naked bottom. Surely it was not when he was born. It is awfully sad and thrilling at once, and he must apologise to God for a lambent moment of hatred in Johanna's direction for ruining his sermon. He shares these thoughts with no one.

Failing the stones, Phillip tries another the following week, the one he has practised with John, who has been noticeably absent lately.

My father told me one thing of the saints that has stayed with me, says Phillip, choosing to sit instead of stand, and taking off his sweeping black cassock. He watches Johanna Lynch and hopes she does not show him her fanny again. Have any of you heard of Virgil? He is the patron saint of all the Irish, more especially the far-flung Irish. I've not known many churches named for him. I suppose that isn't much of a surprise. Those still living in Ireland and Europe have little need of a saint who cares for the wayward traveller. They still know the feeling of home. They've not had to try plant roots in hungry soil. My father told me that Virgil believed in a round Earth long before we sent ships west to find out. He went further than those who simply claimed the world had another side. He claimed that people lived there. In him God has given us a relative to pray to, someone who knew that there must have been a darker side to the world, and that one day we would know the displeasure of living on it.

Phillip had thought if he gave them hope of a future state it might salvage something of their dignity, but as he scours his papers writ in Irish letters, he begins to think the sermon about Virgil much more depressing than it is hopeful.

The passage of 20 hot sea days carries them to the week of Christmas. Phillip has extinguished his desire for medicinal rum. He hears rumours from Ellen that prisoners are lying with the captain and first mate. She hears these things from Isabella Irving, although close-lipped Isabella will not tell them to Phillip herself. Phillip cannot reproach the captain. He fears seriously that he will be cast off the ship if he does. He feels trapped on a floating brothel, a barrel in the vast unknown of the Atlantic Ocean.

At Christmas, Creagh allows a few gallons of rum to go missing and Phillip notices that the sailors openly practise debauchery on the deck. He clutches his sermon sheets and ruins them between two hands. He carries his sores in silence until Ellen and Isabella come to collect his linens.

You have greater concerns to go grey for, says Isabella for the first time. Her words burst out in the middle of one of Phillip's complaints to Ellen. Do not lay awake fretting about the sharpers of the crew that connyfogle us. She takes her hard-worn hands and scrunches her breasts with them. A woman in this outfit can think of 10 things worse than blowing the grounsils with a mariner. Your sermons being one of them. In the dark a woman can't see how ugly a sailor is, and she might forget she's being taken to a fucking prison on the empty side of the Earth.

Phillip has no fight with Isabella's honesty, however impotent it makes him feel.

But please, reverend, for Christ's sake worry about the child.

Phillip stands in a moment of silence.

Sophia Nightingale's girl, young Mary Ann. She's ill. But of course, you don't care for the protestant women on-board, do you Mister Conolly? Isabella takes up the laundry and leaves before he can answer her. Phillip turns to Ellen.

Some of the protestant women wonder if you care only for us catholics, she says.

Are they not in the care of James Creagh? Is it my burden to carry two bibles?

Ellen's voice softens. We don't care about which church we were raised in. Mary Ann Nightingale's sick. Leave her alone if you will, if it is so hard for you to speak to a protestant woman. The only good her religion will do her is to pick which end of the cemetery she's buried in when she gets to New South Wales.

Johanna Lynch makes Phillip nervous. She is sitting beside Sophia Nightingale who has a small infant on her breast. The child's skin is jaune and its eyes are closed and stressed. The eyes of an infant should not be creased with worry, thinks Phillip. She also does not cry, which a baby should do often.

Mowat did not want us to preach to any of them, John had said the night before. His words are in Phillip's head as he looks upon the ill child. Let the girl's illness sit on the captain's conscience.

But he has no conscience, John. I cannot preach mercy and deny a mother prayer, Phillip had argued. Do you not feel the guilt of the old country? It is the very segregation we volunteered to get away from.

You preach like a protestant, John sniped. You extract whatever meaning you choose from the Word of God. You forget the rules. I don't know what you're hoping for, but the world won't make it that way.

It is better that they receive the Word, however doctored, than nothing at all. Phillip thinks these words now.

Phillip sits with the women and does not preach. He prays over Mary Ann as Sophia asks him to. His words of intervention, given over a protestant child, feel like the new shoots of spring. The frail creature opens her eyes once, revealing dark orbs inherited from her unknown father. The scant light of whale wax candles shines on Sophia's mousy nest of hair. Her eyes are the lightest blue. They remind Phillip of his own sister.

Mary Ann is four months old, she says. Sophia's voice is faint but hard. I do not want her to die, she whispers. She has not been baptised.

One by one the women leave their company until only Phillip and Sophia are in the cell with the little girl. Phillip shrugs away the discomfort of a woman's singular company. He continues to pray until Sophia touches his sleeve.

Reverend, can you sing?

Any creature *can* sing. Do I sing well? Phillip lets his silence answer. Better than Creagh, he says after a while.

Sophia elicits a soft smile. Sing.

Phillip hums initially. He begins in timid Irish tones before raising his voice to English.

Be thou my vision ... o Lord of my heart. Naught be all else to me, save that thou art. Thou my best thought, by day or by night. Waking or sleeping, thy presence my light.

Sophia does not know the words, but as his flat voice grows she lifts it with her own formless murmur.

Riches I heed not, nor men's empty praise, thou mine inheritance, now and always. Thou and thou only, first in my heart. High King of Heaven, my treasure thou art.

Phillip visits Sophia every day, without a care for the regard of other women or the eyes of the sailors. Sophia asks him what the word croppy means.

It is a slight. Some prot—some *people* call catholics that name. The old rebels of the rising in '98 used to crop their hair in protest to the powdered wigs English aristocrats wore. It bothers me only a little. My country is in such a state of disrepair I hoped this ship would take me away from it.

Your country and mine, says Sophia.

What of Mary Ann's father? Phillip asks, changing the destination of their dialogue, not lightly.

Jack lives, if that is what you're asking. His last gift to me was Mary Ann. I carried her with me into gaol. She was born there. I do not think he knows. Sophia's china eyes are wet but they do not cry. She may never know any place but prisons.

Hogwash, says Phillip. He scorns prison as replacement for a lying-in hospital, and for the child their only flavour of life. Phillip's humanity is wounded by it. He says to himself: I will not let a prison ship be her mortuary.

Not for the last time he takes the child in his arms. He covers her in the folds of his heavy woollen coat so that her face is not smothered but her body concealed. He joins his hands together inside the billowing sleeves of his cassock. He carries Mary Ann in this way for hours every day in the open air, singing mildly to her and telling her that the salt air will heal her. He does not spend evenings with John anymore.

The curfew is in shambles. The sailors come and go as they please. But they do not go near Sophia Nightingale. Ellen Molloy tells Phillip it is out of fear. She says they do not want to anger Phillip. Phillip tells her she is being hyperbolic. She rolls her eyes at his big words.

Even Creagh is worried by you, she says. He is an old fool that no prisoner will touch, but he tells the sailors he is abstaining from lying with a woman for fear of his soul. Together they laugh. He thinks you will damn him, Ellen says.

Phillip's laughter dies away. He should not be afraid of me, Phillip says gravely.

The memory of their laughter seems to mock Phillip in the days after when he sees a prisoner stumble from Creagh's quarters in the forecastle, her demure dress hastily buttoned. He can tolerate the demise of the sailors, but Creagh carries a prayer book in his hands – his perjury violates the crucifix on Phillip's neck. In anger he seeks out John for support, but he cannot find him in the 'tween-deck. Evening is falling and the women retire to their messes.

Johanna may know where he is, says Isabella, looking about the mess where only Sophia and Ellen remain. She promised to fetch fresh linens when I was done, says Isabella gesturing towards the cargo hold.

Phillip goes alone. His feet echo in the cargo hold as their soles clap the iron rungs. The shaft of light from the hatch is poorly, but it is enough to confirm his suspicions. There are no words in English, Irish or Latin for the disgrace.

The Reverend John Terry fires to his feet, collecting from his ankles a pair of white breeches. Johanna does not seem offended. She seems amused. She is naked. In the half darkness, Phillip takes a long moment as he spreads his eyes over her body – her neck, her breasts, the insides of her legs. Johanna lays on her side with her head supported by a cocked elbow and hand. Her green eyes do more than undress Phillip – they take apart his flesh as well. Phillip knows it is a sin but he stares at her anyway. At least he can admit he is a hypocrite.

He chases John up the ladder into the 'tween-deck. The women's audience is a shame.

You cannot judge me, John shrieks as he tucks in the tails of his shirt. Everyone speaks of how you lie with that married woman Nightingale.

Her child is ill you fool. Has the depravity of this lawless, floating island worn away your years of instruction already? What of the college seminary? What of our holy orders? Do they mean nothing to you John? Phillip feels his eyes burning. He cannot drench himself of the vision of Johanna's naked body, laid there on piles of canvas like a drawing in charcoal. Not even archangels have the power of a priest, and here you are rutting on a folded sail! He swipes a damning finger.

There are greater evils that we will face, Phillip.

Phillip leaves John in the middle of the deck. He walks around him. John yells after him. You must be poorly trained if this breaks you!

Who has it broken, John? Phillip turns sharply and draws a straight finger.

★ ★ ★

There is no choice but to reinstate strict curfew. Captain Mowat cannot let the argument of the priests go unnoticed, although he does a fine job of ignoring James Creagh's adultery. Phillip avoids them all – Mowat, Creagh and especially John. He dedicates his weeks to Mary Ann's care. It takes the remaining months at sea, but as they breach the waters of Van Diemen's Land, with the distant smudge of coast on the bloody east horizon, Mary Ann regains her colour. She cries every other day.

Phillip knows that his collapsed brotherhood with John will stay on-board the *Janus*. In a terse moment they agree that Phillip will alight in Hobart-town and John will go on to Sydney. Phillip martyrs himself when he says to John, There is not enough room in Van Diemen's Land for two hypocrites.

It bites him that he cannot cast John before the retribution of a council or a court, but to do so would damage the bond he has with the women; he will not break the one thing he has built.

It would also shine a painful light on the narrow pupil of his smarting heart, which keeps buried sins he would rather not touch.

If he could confide in John he might confess them, as a priest may only confess to another priest, but in Van Diemen's Land he will be the only one. He cannot confess to himself.

Mowat will not compromise Phillip's character. Phillip knows this. The captain is so deep in misconduct that there will be no report of his wroth in the colonies and no word of his preaching to two congregations. It will be a new leaf. Jesus, thinks Phillip, how many new leaves before the book is done?

He stands with Sophia, Mary Ann in her arms, upon the quarter deck in the late morning. The retreating folds of the green shore bring to mind the west coast of Clare. He was a young priest there, where he flogged a surly horse on the ribbon of road between villages which respected only the frigid wilderness of the wide Atlantic. The *Janus* bends around the deep skirt of the peninsula, now facing nor'west towards Hobart-town. Sophia raises her free hand to the dour pillars of the pipe organ rocks which rise from the sea unfettered.

It almost makes the journey of nine thousand miles worthwhile, don't you think? she says, shifting Mary Ann.

Phillip cannot agree. His thoughts are chased and eaten by God's strange humour. The rocks remind Phillip of the charred honeycomb coast of the north of his country. How can such a foreign place look like home? Is the antipodes of a place its fraternal twin? He thinks, with disenchanted grief, that Ireland has not perished under the waves – they have brought it with them.

CONOLLY

Hobart-town, April 1821 A.D.

Phillip has not heard Irish voices sing since his last service in Ireland. Even then they had sung in English. This morning, on the last Saturday of April, as he stands upon the gallows, the convicts sing to no music. Only the keening of prison chains accompanies their voices. It is only Irish voices singing, and they sing to one of their own.

Phillip looks into the crowded street. Behind the thick weave of people, he sees the lieutenant-governor on the steps of the court house, who he first met upon arrival Christmas last. Lieutenant-governor Sorell is shorter than his companion, the governor in chief Lachlan Macquarie, who has descended from Sydney to inspect the state of his southernmost colony. Phillip looks at the Irish convict, connected to the gibbet by a rope, who has just kicked off his boots, one of them flinging over the wall and into the crowd. Shouts and whistles arouse him. Take me, Jack! he cries, spitting. It is a first-rate welcome for the governor, thinks Phillip.

He met the protestant reverend, Robert Knopwood, early in January, who stands with him on the gallows – there are enough protestants being executed today as well. They take it in turns to climb the stair and minster to the damned before watching them go down to the shadows beneath the platform. Knopwood's words cling to the inside of his head: *If you cannot save their souls, at least keep them quiet. A governor told me that years ago.*

Phillip tries to comprehend the faces of the officials beneath the eave of the court house but he cannot. It doesn't matter. He knows he has failed.

The singing burgeons. More chains join the choir. The present Irishman is lifted by the hooded hangman to the drop. He does not seem to care. Phillip comes close to him and touches the knot of the noose on his shoulder. His prayers are drowned out by the town chorus:

Now I am one that never lied to you,

And I never yet took a bribe;

I carry off the youth and the elders,

And the strongest man alive;

I take them with me before the Only Son,

Reading lists of their sins in hand;

And I will take you with me, my fair, sprightly John;

Dispute no more, come along.

Do not hurry to the end of your life. Phillip's voice is impotent in his own ears.

Fuck off. The prisoner's face is lit up by a savage grin. His eyes are intoxicated by the crowd. The soldiers below cannot stop the singing.

When the Irishman is dead, Phillip leans against the timber leg of the gallows stage, waiting for Knopwood to pray for his last. The song in the street has meandered into nothing. The Irish only sing for their own. Phillip remembers the words sung at a funeral of his childhood. The convicts have brought the old dirge all this way. He feels the timber stress and quiver and hears the whip–crack of the taut noose. He hears Knopwood's hurried prayers.

Phillip thinks it perfectly within the tastes of the colony's gentry that Sorell should host a party after the hanging. He is apprehended by Knopwood and a young girl in the court house square.

The governor is entertaining a host at the house of Mister and Mis'ess Birch, Knopwood says glibly. Governor will want you there.

Phillip wonders which governor. He would rather decline, but he knows he has no choice.

The Birch mansion is a slender turret of pink bricks overlooking the high bank of the street a few hundred yards from the gaol grounds. Its tall windows look south to the bay with the marshy burial ground distant. Knopwood tells Phillip that if he is ever lost or called for, that Phillip will likely find him sleeping in the punchbowl in this house. The drunk reverend might be the first protestant minister Phillip has liked.

Sorell is dressed up in all the finery of an officer, with curls of white hair at his temples that brighten his vaulting eyes. Knopwood and Phillip retrieve his attention in the upstairs hall as he leads the party to Birch's own grand dining room. Phillip is aware that government house is so dilapidated that Sorell has moved in with the Birchs. When Sorell sees Phillip he retreats from the head of the column and shakes his hand heartily. A woman lingers with him.

Knopwood hobbles ahead towards the statue of a man which must be the governor in chief. Knopwood presses his cane against the dining room door to clear the way for Governor Macquarie, unaware that it is the spry young girl behind him actually holding the door open. Phillip appreciates the comedy of a fat old man and a child holding the door for a decorated soldier. Six others go with them.

Colonel, Phillip says simply, hoping the blundering display at the gallows does not come up in conversation.

Some show today, remarks Sorell. Phillip cringes. He looks for a convenient change of topic. While he has known Sorell now four months, he has not met the smiling woman behind him, who he takes to be his wife.

Mis'ess Sorell, he addresses with a bow. Why has the good governor kept me from your company, these four months?

The lady's smile vanishes. Phillip notices Sorell's eyes dart to the woman's. Phillip thinks he can see Robert Knopwood, cane upon the door ahead, laughing into a handkerchief.

Sorell's returning beam is courteous only. He puts a hand on Phillip's back, between his shoulders. Capital to have you, reverend. Capital. Shall we take after the others? Mister Birch is a capital drinker and I'll not give him the head start.

Phillip meets some of the others, but not all, in the grand dining room. He only shakes the hand of Mister Birch in passing, who is an eccentric puffin of a man dressed in a knee-length green coat. He must have been an adult when his wife, Sarah, was a child, thinks Phillip. He knows James Scott, who is one of the royal surgeons, and is introduced to his betrothed Lucy.

Phillip relaxes in his seat and toasts providence with a hearty drink. He is seated beside Robert Knopwood; if he were seated beside that Lieutenant Cuthbertson across the table he thinks he might drown himself in the punch instead. That lieutenant looks like the four limbs of boredom.

James's Lucy is the daughter of the former governor, did you know? Knopwood asks Phillip, his fleshy red nose hanging like a pear. He explains that her father is now away from the colony.

The commons called him Mad Tom. By *God* he could hold his liquor in gallons. I've known worse men who weren't boozers, says Knopwood. Macquarie despises him. As Knopwood speaks, Phillip arraigns the faces at the table.

Macquarie sits at the head with Sorell at his right hand. Below the lieutenant-governor is James Scott followed by the unimpressive Mis'ess Sorell and Lucy Davey. Knopwood is next and Phillip sits between him and his young attendant. Up the other flank of the table he sees colourful Birch and his wife and his sea captain, James Kelly, and finally, between Kelly and the governor in chief, the Irish lieutenant of the 48th regiment. Phillip's wandering glance intercepts the keen direction of Cuthbertson's eyes; they are intense and grey. Phillip does not know why he feels a phantom draught down his neck. Macquarie and Sorell and Scott speak together. Cuthbertson lowers his eyes to their union, releasing Phillip's.

Who is the woman I met in the hall? Phillip asks Knopwood with discretion.

O, you mean the woman you addressed as mis'ess? Knopwood replies with an uncomfortably public voice. Mistress, more like. You were half right calling her mis'ess, except that she is another man's mis'ess. Furthermore, Mis'ess *Sorell* is at home in England suffering with the lieutenant-governor's children.

Phillip wonders what Macquarie thinks of a colony where even the governor is an adulterer.

Macquarie may look cordial with Sorell at a dinner party, says Knopwood spying up the table, but be assured he thinks we're all drunks. Blame Lucy's old man for that.

Surely Macquarie doesn't think ill of drinking men?

You don't understand, Phillip, Davey put it down. Or should I say, he never put it down. Knopwood chuckles. I will give you some advice for free, he goes on, pulling Phillip into the odour of his breath, Davey drank with the commoners and they loved him for it. Buffoon or not, a man loved is a man feared. If all a man does is inspire fear, the people beneath him will rise up to spite him, even if it means their necks.

Knopwood dashes his eyes across the glassware to the coats at the head of the table. Bear that in mind when tending to your flock. Phillip thinks the reverend drunk. If you are loved by your people, they will not want to do wrong. I am become all things to all men that I may win them for Christ. Letter to the Philippians. My girl! Knopwood adulates as his young attendant returns to the table with not merely a glass but a decanter. Have you properly met my daughter, Betty?

You have a daughter?

Yes, I have a daughter. She is not my flesh and blood, Knopwood says softer, kissing the young girl's hand, but then Caesar was adopted and didn't that mean nix. Betty looks favourably at Phillip.

Reverend Knopwood will be more blind than usual this evening, Betty, Phillip says. Take care walking him home.

Betty leans in, squeaking: The more he drinks the heavier he becomes. I regularly roll him to Cottage Green like a barrel.

Knopwood slaps his knee and nearly spills his drink.

When the decanter is empty Phillip asks after the servants. He is pointed to a platter of drinks by the door. He carries his tumbler to the line of carafes on a long silver plate at the entry. As he approaches he sees a woman peering through a crack in the door. When her eyes fall on Phillip her face retreats. Watchful of his steps, Phillip leaves his glass on the plate and pushes quietly into the hall.

Johanna! his voice is hoarse with whisper. The servant stops. Water jumps from the jug in her hand. Phillip hurries ahead.

The woman sets her vessel aside and turns. Her eyes are luminous, even in the dim hall. Phillip eases towards her. As he draws closer she casts her arms around his neck. Phillip feels her breath on his ear. He stumbles back. Their hands fall into a limp clasp and then nothing at all. In the faint light Phillip perceives a glassy look in her eye. She does not smile.

They said one of the catholic priests was going to Sydney, her voice is not as tart as Phillip remembers. I hoped it was not you.

The creaking dining room door breaks them apart. Johanna Lynch collects her water jug and plashes back to the larder. Phillip feels suddenly drunk. He sees Betty on the threshold of the dining room. She looks directly at him with an inquisitive eye.

It is a month before Phillip goes looking for her.

In the intervening time he is called to hangings at Launceston and George-town, settlements like gull shit on the northward rocks of the island. Nine men fall to their deaths, about half Irish Roman catholic. All thieves. He feels stretched thin himself as he rides the long lonely road back to Hobart.

In Hobart Phillip chances across Sarah Birch in the street where he asks her if one of her servants turned up his rosary beads. She says she cannot remember, to which Phillip says he misplaced them in the dining room about a month ago.

Ann is the head maidservant, says Mis'ess Birch. She would know. She lives in a skilling over east by the bond store. She has a young child. If you call she may be in.

She has a child?

To a man named Cavanagh. They aren't married – Sarah Birch cannot abstain from gossip – I pity the baby. I said to Thomas, come dear let us employ this wretched girl.

Phillip is polite enough to smile and bow before taking off on brisk heels.

By the banks of the town rivulet a hamlet of shanties frown at one another across a straight track. Phillip draws suspicious looks from idle prisoners. He recognises none of them. It must be queer for a priest in black to walk this muddy track.

Behind one sod hut with a skillion off the side, Phillip sees a woman pulling on a clothes line. A string of dresses and shirts are suspended between the flat, green roof and a gum tree with roots thick in the clay bank of the creek. Phillip watches her a long while.

Can I fetch you something? A man emerges from the dark covering of the lean-to.

Phillip is caught off guard. The prisoner recognises him when he speaks, but his tone does not brighten: Reverend. Can I fetch you something, reverend?

Phillip sees Johanna pivot and meet his face. He cannot read her countenance. She disappears inside the sod hut.

Are you Cavanagh? Phillip asks the man. I am looking for Johanna. I misplaced a personal article at the house of Thomas Birch.

Christ, Cavanagh swears. Are you calling Ann a thief?

Steady John. The voice is Johanna's. Phillip is relieved to see her shape. Do not give yourself a bad heart. Go inside.

John Cavanagh is sluggish. His eyes rake across Phillip's figure and then he is gone.

We have well-practised manners now, do we not. Johanna's hands are on her hips.

Is it Ann now? asks Phillip.

Are you keeping up with the Birchs now? Johanna walks away to the rivulet. Phillip follows her.

It feels longer than five months, he says to her. Do you have a child?

Yes. Little Brigid.

To him? Phillip knows it cannot be Cavanagh's child. It has been five months. Is the child not christened? Phillip asks when Johanna does not speak.

Until now we have not had a priest to bless marriages or christen infants, bejesus.

Tell me about the girl, Phillip asks, putting away the old memories of their voyage and paying mind to the coarseness of his tongue. Johanna's haggard face is gilt with a little light. Phillip enjoys her smile, but he cannot hold himself at bay when Johanna collects the girl from inside.

She is newborn, Phillip says, touching the soft red forehead with a gentle finger. Do not tell me now this was an immaculate conception.

He wants to ask who is the girl's father, but he is frightened Johanna will not know. Instead he asks her: Will you marry

Cavanagh, now that I am here?

Johanna does not spare a moment to think. I do not love him, but a woman is a prostitute without a man in her house. He is a cruel man, but he fights off other cruel men and he has not harmed Brigid.

Are we making the best the enemy of the good, are we Johanna?

What is good, reverend? Have I another man to live with? Will you take me in?

Her question startles Phillip. He knows she does not mean it, but a part of his mind disbelieves him. He flounders.

I cannot be married, he says. He thinks briefly of his father's ghost. I am married to the church.

Johanna throws her head back. We do not have a catholic church yet in Hobart-town. One cannot be married to a bride that does not live in the same country. Johanna's sneer, the sneer Phillip remembers, relents a little as she asks a surprising question: I do not suppose you will christen Brigid, will you?

Phillip takes her hands in his. He shakes a little, but is glad he does it. Will you fetch me a bowl? he says.

When Johanna returns she brings Brigid to the creek on her hip. A chipped bowl is in her spare hand.

This is the Reverend Mister Conolly, Johanna says lightly to her child whose face is covered in an angry red rash. The infant is not bothered by the flakes of skin that snow over her bulging eyes. Phillip takes the bowl from Johanna and lowers it into the creek. He raises it to the child and sprinkles water onto the infant's head. The baby does not cry. Phillip prays over the water in the bowl. Johanna asks if it will turn into wine. Phillip says he is a priest, not a miracle worker.

Brigid Cavanagh, he says, I baptise you in the name of the Father and of the Son and of the Holy Ghost. Remember that God is with you always, even unto the end of the world. Phillip signs his body with the cross.

Cavanagh is not inside when Phillip and Johanna go in. Johanna gives him hard biscuits and small circles of bread with jam and dripping ladled over.

Where is Sophia? the question is as abrupt to Phillip as it is to Johanna.

Johanna seems disappointed by the question. She works for the government, Johanna informs perfunctorily. I hear by the bye she has been assigned to one of the constables—Hellings I think is his name. She does not have a man as I have, if you are interested.

You are wicked, Johanna. I think only of her little girl.

Silence spreads between them. Phillip feels the discomfort of a lost moment. His legs are restless. He reaches for his watch.

Leave the watch, says Johanna with surprising tenderness. You had better get going before John returns.

Phillip stands. He intends to bow but Johanna plants her lips on his cheek before he can.

Do not tell your bride I kissed you when she gets built.

★ ★ ★

Phillip never forgot Johanna, not in four months, but seeing her again has touched up her image in his mind. He thinks of her words as he gives mass in a general store to nine free catholics. In the course of prayer he thinks that he is no good to any prisoner if he only ministers to them before they die. He thinks of the baby he has baptised, and he wonders about Sophia's child.

Do you know a Constable Hellings? Phillip asks Knopwood after church.

I've been gathering dust here for two decades, Conolly, I know everybody, says Knopwood with a glass of brandy.

You are quite the dusty fellow, says Phillip.

Why do you ask about Hellings?

I am looking for a woman, Phillip says.

Why, Hellings is a man.

Relief, says Phillip. It is his crown servant I'm looking her. Sophia and I were transported together.

Knopwood's blotchy face is kind. Mary Ann, he remarks. Do you know the child?

She was deathly ill on the journey over. I wondered if she yet lived.

Aye, she lives. I could take you there this afternoon if you wish. Knopwood arrives at an instant decision. Betty! he shouts in the parlour room of his house. Show me my cane!

Together they roll by horse-drawn car from Knopwood's home at Cottage Green to Hobart-town, the glister of the bay below their right wheel. When they arrive in the neighbourhood of servant houses which foils the straight church-road into narrow lanes, Phillip sees a small green window with a fair-haired woman inside it. He leaves Knopwood's buggy and approaches the house timidly. He knocks. His sister Nora opens the door.

Phillip has not thought of what to say. Sophia places both hands over her mouth. She leaves sooty black hand prints on her face. Phillip looks down at her chimney-sweep smock and the iron brush upon the door jamb. She fusses over a rag, trying to clean her cheeks and nose. Phillip follows her watery delighted laugh indoors.

He walks up to the hearth and rubs a finger across the bricks. He gives his face a black streak to save Sophia the embarrassment. She laughs again. Now she cries. Tears streak through the soot. Phillip can hear the murmurings of a young child. He corners an open doorway and sees Mary Ann waddling on the ground dragging a beaten doll behind her. Phillip looks again at Mary Ann's mother. After five months he is still astonished at how contagious his sister's apparition is.

I am so glad to see her walk, Phillip says.

It is because of you. Sophia is distracted by the sound of a horse outside. She collects Mary Ann with her doll and Phillip joins her in the front room. Did you come with Bobby Knopwood? she asks, peering through the small green window.

Is that what the people call him?

That is what his *parishioners* call him. He is a good sort. His daughter is beautiful.

His adopted daughter, Phillip feels compelled to add.

Yes, well I suppose it is convenient for a man of the cloth to adopt a child, considering he may have none himself.

How will I see you? Phillip asks Sophia tenderly.

By knocking on my door. Constable Hellings is a good man. I want you to visit Mary Ann as frequently as you like.

Phillip looks through the small green window to be sure there are no witnesses, then he raises his arms. Sophia fits herself inside them. For the first time Phillip feels that Hobart-town is where he belongs.

CUTHBERTSON

Van Diemen's Land, 1821 A.D.

Lieutenant John Cuthbertson thinks that although laughter is a display of weakness, sometimes a smile can be as menacing as a scowl.

This is why he smiles at the prisoners as they tramp past him. They seem disquieted by it. They tramp with the road tools upon their shoulders. On the other side of the path is Private William Pugh, sitting on a stump with an axe in his lap. The pebble he scrapes up its silver edge runs like nails on slate. Cuthbertson looks at the axe and he looks at Pugh and he looks at the prisoners and he smiles.

The private is head and shoulders above other soldiers. He is built like a butcher's rack. He is daunting with an axe in his lap.

It is not standard issue, and it is not very sharp, but Cuthbertson allows him to keep it because of what it does to the prisoners. They all know the story: Pugh is the one that cut off Michael Howe's head.

That is why the prisoners do not sing anymore as they work. They look at Big Bill and remember that it is he who cut off the head of the worst bushranger of the troubles years ago. They know that if they step out of line Bill will cut off their heads to save him the worry of irons.

Cuthbertson knows Pugh would be hanged if he did this, but the convicts may not. Most of them were working the same road six months earlier when Pugh had blown the prisoner Thomas Atkinson's hand clean off.

That is what the prisoners believe. But Cuthbertson reaches inside his jacket, feels for the shape of his old East India pattern pistol, and knows the truth. He has never missed a shot with it.

It is an heirloom of his father, a protestant man, a king's man. How many rebels his father killed with it, he cannot know. Cuthbertson comprehends the irony of Pearce stealing the pistol from him – it is the very pistol that killed his kind. He was told by a captain once that it was three pounds of dead weight for an infantryman to carry a cavalry pistol, but it has never weighed him down.

The other soldiers tried to stop the bleeding but their efforts were wasted when Atkinson died in coagulated gravel. Cuthbertson remembers the day vividly, the 2nd or 3rd of May. Atkinson had appeared with six others, five of them English, the other that Irish misfit named Alexander Pearce. How a runt from Monaghan came to fall in with bushrangers, Cuthbertson does not know. He should have pushed for the magistrates to send him to Newcastle a year ago when he was caught with that forged note, instead of a sheep run up the country. Pearce is the kind who will never be reformed. He should be in Newcastle by now, along with the others. It is where all secondary offenders are transported, a place of stricter punishment.

Pugh had fired off a warning shot, but the prisoners scattered. Cuthbertson saw some of them run for the trees and would not let them get away. If they hated labour so much, then what he did to Atkinson with his pistol was a mercy.

The second shot was his. While Atkinson expired, Cuthbertson ordered Pugh to collect the musket Pearce had dropped. He checked the chamber and fired a single ball into the air.

The prisoner fired first, he said to Pugh.

He wonders if it ever crosses Pugh's mind that Michael Howe was once a soldier. The two of them may have fought in the same wars Cuthbertson has served in. It is remarkable to Cuthbertson that both could arrive at blows in Van Diemen's Land, two men of the same kind, ferried to the other side of the world, yet dressed in such different coats.

Lieutenant Cuthbertson, sir. Sergeant Waddy retrieves the officer from his thoughts. The governor is in town. He has asked for you.

Cuthbertson looks away across the river to Hobart-town. He wonders what the governor could want. Promptly he collects his grey mare from a nearby ensign and leaves his command with the sergeant. Without a second thought he spurs his horse with a clip of heels.

Bronze shelducks sail through the air as Cuthbertson crosses into town. He cannot mistake the governor's party, readying a whaleboat on the quay.

Lieutenant! beckons the governor, raising his hands. The governor's secretary lets off a shot from a long carbine. How is your aim? the governor asks.

Cuthbertson brings his horse to a sudden halt, Sharper than Mister Robinson's, he says loud enough for the secretary to hear.

Good. Sorell passes him a rifle. Bring me a swan.

There are black birds with bloody red beaks in the shallow water between the shoal and Hunter Island.

Cuthbertson checks the pan. It is already powdered. Ball? he asks, holding the flintlock gently. Sorell nods. Tipping his head with satisfaction Cuthbertson faces the water. He presents the musket and fires into a rising flight of elegant swans.

Boast after action, says Robinson with the sting of comeuppance.

They are on the island, Sorell reports, gazing over the water. None had fallen to Cuthbertson's shot. He grips the musket firm to evince his frustration. Into the boat, Sorell orders. We will shoot them from the water.

Cuthbertson notices how paltry the flock of swans is as the oars pull them closer to the island.

There were many more two years ago, Robinson answers without explanation for their disappearance.

What do you know of Macquarie Harbour? Sorell asks

Cuthbertson as though he has plucked the thought from air.

James Kelly tells me it is far to the west. Cuthbertson recalls a dinner at Thomas Birch's many months ago. He tells me it is an isolated inlet much larger than Port Jackson, but that a ship must get by the narrowest channel to sail inside. Mountains and deep valleys and country which has never been mapped lay between that harbour and here. Thomas Birch has been made rich by all the pine he has hauled away from that place.

Sorell agrees. Kelly told me the same, he says. There are thousands of black swans there. He regards the animals which fold their wings away on Hunter Island. Coal too. Kelly named an island there for Mister Birch's wife. I think it would make the ideal penitentiary.

A station for secondary offenders, sir?

Precisely.

The boat strafes within firing distance. Sorell offers Cuthbertson the flintlock once more but Cuthbertson declines. He rises again, feeling the uncertain wobble of the boat beneath him. He takes a cartridge from Robinson which he tears open with his teeth. He opens the pan of his pistol and covers it with powder, retaining a cold, lead ball in his mouth.

Filled with gunpowder, Cuthbertson locks the pan and holds the pistol high. The remaining gunpowder he pours into the bore hole. He punches the ball and cartridge paper deep into the throat of the pistol with a short loading rod.

What of the prisoners we send to Newcastle? he asks the governor.

Any prisoner under crimes of secondary offence is being held here. It has been a desire of mine for some time to keep them in the colony. It seems a wanton expense to send them all the way to Newcastle when we can have them work on our own island.

Cuthbertson thinks of Pearce and Atkinson dead upon the orange ground. He holds his pistol to the damp spring air and wonders when he will fight again. He recalls Spain and France and Portugal. Talavera is on his mind. He savours the distant flavour of all those battles. A bushranger is not a fight. He feels wasted on the nursery of criminals. But here he is, in a boat with the lieutenant-governor of Van Diemen's Land. His privileged company says something for his years of toil. He closes one eye and the shot rings true.

Cuthbertson enjoys mild applause as he returns to a bench. A swan's mangled body is tossed in the surf. The sky is cast with the shade of frightened wings. He looks at the governor whose lips are pregnant with near speech.

I intend to establish a penal colony at Macquarie Harbour, Sorell announces. I spoke with Macquarie about this in April and he agrees. All I need is a magistrate. Sorell reaches beneath his seat and takes up a crescent bundle of cloth. I do not have a badge of office to give you. I can only give you a guarantee that your achievements will recommend future promotion. And I can give you this.

He passes the bundle to Cuthbertson. Beneath the layer of cloth is a crescent of brass metal with the royal coat of arms embossed. That neck plate must be 25 years old, he says. I had that when I was a captain.

Cuthbertson holds his own reflection in the plate. It is not an orphan boy from county Tyrone who looks back at him. He can bear the Irish name of Cuthbertson when it follows the word lieutenant, but if it followed captain? He could forgive it entirely.

While the plate does not grant him the rank of captain, the promise of promotion is enough. His decorations will buy him status, and with status he can barter for respect. Then perhaps one day it will be him handing a metal neck plate to a lieutenant. Perhaps one day he will take a wife and his children will forget they ever came from Irish stock. But he has many miles to go before that decorated day.

What say you? Sorell asks at last.

Cuthbertson covers the plate. He holds his pistol before him. Robison drags the sopping lump of swan into the midst of the whaleboat. If there are a thousand swans at Macquarie Harbour, says Cuthbertson, I had better practise my aim.

ACT TWO

CUTHBERTSON

Macquarie Harbour, 1822 A.D.

The water smokes like it is burning, but Cuthbertson knows if he were to fall in he would freeze before he drowned.

He expects the worst prisoners will attempt to swim when they effect their inevitable escapes. That is why they are chained. They do not understand it is for their benefit.

One hundred convicts under his power. They are the scotched corrupted likeness of a working party which an explorer might take with him. To keep them in line Cuthbertson has seventeen infantrymen – hardly an army. Only seventeen soldiers to control a hundred.

There are 66 convicts with him on-board the *Sophia*, and half his lieutenant's guard. Cuthbertson fights the fear that the others have drowned. The second ship, the *Prince Leopold*, was dragged away from their company in a tempest off the south coast and she has not arrived. Most of the skilled workers are with her, along with sawn timber and nails, and the other half of his lieutenant's guard. It is a wicked omen.

A spirit of agonised disquiet swells in the chambers and floods the deck of the *Sophia*. It touches everything with a colour more foul. Tensions are pinched tighter. The absence of the *Prince Leopold* haunts the crew. The castration of the rising sun by the impervious white breath of the beating west sea tells them they have sailed into thrashing waters which devour time. Even the shore moves and disappears in phantoms. The stretching sounds of leather and shrinking timber-joins give the effect that the brig is chattering. It treads with fright towards the narrow maw of the harbour.

Kelly, Cuthbertson calls the captain to the bow.

James Kelly raises a seeking hand, as though he can feel the rocks which pierce the gloom ahead. The ship's bowsprit points to a narrow passage in between. The strait may only be 80 yards across, he says, but it is not so shallow that I cannot sail *Sophie* through.

Orange teeth represent each gate of the harbour, serrated stones stained with lichen. There is a space between them of three cricket pitches, but Cuthbertson fears the strait's depth. Kelly licks a finger and points at the sky.

There is a small island rising over portside, and to the starboard mainland. The dark sea swells in treacherous waves. Kelly tells Cuthbertson the narrow passage between the orange teeth is their only course, but Cuthbertson is tempted by white waves which he can see behind the small black island.

We will be caught on sandy flats over there, says Kelly. He

tosses his hand towards the wider water. It looks easy, but the easy way is not always the true way.

Cuthbertson's scribbler, the convict clerk John Douglas, stands nearby. He has ferret's eyes which are shrunken by a snoutish nose. He is murmuring scripture: Enter ye in at the strait gate: for wide is the gate, and broad is the way, that leadeth to destruction, and many there be which go in thereat …

Quiet Douglas. Private Reynolds, Cuthbertson calls out to a young man who rakes fingers through blonde hair. Rouse the prisoners.

Presently the 66 convicts are herded together on deck. Reynolds and the other soldiers bound the convict mass in a tenuous oval of their bodies. Among the prisoners stand 22 whose skills, and not their sins, have sent them to Macquarie Harbour. For sins there are 44 in chains − 44 incorrigible beasts who lay upon the kentledge in the bowels of the brig. They do not have beds like common men and women. They are beneath common men and women.

He has heard the rumours: China, the far Pacific, South America; rumours of where they are destined. The manure of these rumours sprouts the stalks of tales which grow thick and fat when watered by the rain. They are afraid of what they do not know. Now Cuthbertson introduces them to their prison.

You are not on holiday, he starts with a carrying voice. The tiring breath of the ocean numbs his face. He does not tell them that they lay west of settlement, lest they be encouraged to escape. You have come to the end of the world. Here the governor desires you to work as a consequence of your crimes. And work you shall.

He takes a naval whip from Private Reynolds, a barbed lash with dormant flails so heavy they do not stir in the wind.

There is no escape from this harbour. Do not contemplate escape. Contemplate your freedom only by your labour. Beyond those gates – he points the lash to the bow – is the prison that God made. The shackles you wear are your own creations. With your error comes the lash, and the hand upon the whip is your own: no punishment comes unasked for.

Cuthbertson lays a strike against the foremast. The whip clings with biting scraps of lead.

It is an uneasy childbirth through the strait, which the prisoners have already christened hell's gates, but Kelly has done it before. As the captain opens the sails to the driving wind, Cuthbertson runs his eyes over the landscape as a carpenter feels the grooves of a piece of unmade wood. The world dances in grace notes. Sorell had not lied about the swans. There are black swans in spearheads upon the water, leaving silver streams in the liquid coal. Thousands of them. The natural state of the place is appalling.

The water begins to bleed – with each mile under sail it darkens to a sinister burgundy stain. It is the colour of a whaler's bay, as though a thousand whales have been slaughtered on its beaches.

Cuthbertson's mind is ambushed by the haunting

disappearance of the other brig, and half his lieutenant's guard with it. The *Leopold* won't be sunk, Kelly says honestly. The sea was not rough enough. It was a sailor's sea. The commander of your ship is failed, not the ship herself. *Leopold* will come.

I cannot afford to lose six men, Cuthbertson says quietly. I cannot afford to lose *one* man.

A quiet moment intervenes before Kelly breaks it. Do you think it is true? What Sorell expects about this place? Inescapable?

Cuthbertson lifts his hand to the most immediate mountain. You should know better than any, James. No map knows what lies beyond that mountain. No expedition has ever made tracks across it. If any of these convicts attempt escape, they'll die in that wilderness.

Do you believe that? Kelly asks.

Cuthbertson does not wish to interrogate what he believes and what he does not. No one will escape this place and live, he says.

Ahead, sir. The voice belongs to the navigator Lucas. In the burgundy water to the south lies a dark wooded island. There is a small rock in the harbour beside it with a channel in between. Kelly calls it Sarah Island, but Cuthbertson does not want it to have a name.

Settlement Island, he proclaims with authority. Kelly does not protest.

It is perfect for Sorell's design. A separate island renders bolting almost impossible. As with the other penal colonies, the fungus ergot will be baked into convict bread so that it rots quick on a long journey. Sorell's other orders are clear in Cuthbertson's mind: no tobacco, liquor or comforts of any kind.

He recites the words like scripture: The sameness of occupation, the dreariness of situation, must, if anything will, reform the vicious characters who are sent to you. You must find work and labour, if it only consists of opening cavities and filling them up again. They drop anchor in the island's shallow waters as the bone sky bruises.

At the end of the first day, when he has burned through his tobacco, Cuthbertson retires to his cabin for a quart of Bengal Rum. He does this alone. He thinks the ration the measure of a man. He peers into the finger of rum, a dark swill at the base of his glass. A single ration. It is all that he will drink.

He does not believe in the clouds or the fog that are three draughts and drunkenness. He prefers rather the bright blinding sun that strips away the smoke on the water. The single shot. The enabler. The sharpener of senses. The whetstone. That is his ration. That is his moderation. His control. His power. Other men – the convicts especially – take their grog to numb. Cuthbertson is of the opinion that a man who feels obliged to numb his pain is not a man at all, for a man is one who shoulders pain, who does not closet it up but absorbs it. Wears it on his breast. A man who drinks in excess is a man who is afraid.

Cuthbertson makes clear that they will remain on-board until the *Prince Leopold* arrives, but after only two days his patience expires. His soldiers make camp on the southern tail of the slim beach where the hounds of the western wind are turned back by a rocky lee. When the convicts arrive onshore they are given orders to clear every tree, shrub and fern on the island. They are left in chains. Cuthbertson's soldiers tell those who are without tools, in the absence of the supply ship, to use their own irons to strip the land.

For three days the face of the island is fired like the iron pit of a factory. The sky above is red every night and every morning. Prisoners carve sodden paths away from the wind which is choked with black smoke. Cuthbertson is constantly removing and reshouldering his coat – the chill and heat dance with one another so frequently. In three days the island is naked, except for one fern.

When Cuthbertson comes onto the island to confirm the report, the prisoners plead with him to let them have the fern. It is their only shade from the assailant summer sun, which does not spare its savagery when cold clouds are stripped away. They call it the venerable old treefern. It is like a monument to them.

Cuthbertson sees it. Its broad emerald hands are dark and lime in the dancing light. He does not think mercy is honourable, but this creature has survived the fire, who knows how long it has stood in this place ...

Cuthbertson gives them their fern but does not let them rest with it. All the sawyers are missing with the *Prince Leopold*, so he commands the prisoners to build their own barracks. They build the island's first huts too, out of whatever crude timber is left over from the violent clearing. They are little more than pigeonholes with calico shawls.

Of the timber remaining from the violent clearing, there are long yellow slabs of Huon pine. Cuthbertson ensures these are set aside in a pile of their own. He has brought with him from Hobart-town plans for a schooner which he will build. He touches the brass neck plate on his breast. He will return, when his service is ended, with a ship the quality of which Governor Sorell has never seen. He will give it the governor's name and he will take his promotion from the governor's hand.

He must order the prisoners to cover the Huon pine in leather tarps because the island is washing away. Though it is summer, the place is as wet as it is hot. A squall hits the island and weeps away all its congealed dirt in dangerous slides. The muddy broth clashes with the red sea.

Three weeks pass before Cuthbertson catches sight of a bruised ship's jurymast on the horizon. For a moment he thinks it the premature return of the *Sophia,* which has lately departed for Hobart-town, but his regularly angry mind is soothed as the ship gains size. The *Prince Leopold* has lost its mast.

Captain Chase, he barks as a boat bumps the shore filled with the remaining soldiers of his lieutenant's guard. Tell me: am I desperately early, or are you desperately late? Cuthbertson looks at the coats of his soldiers which are faded pink by the rain and patched with dull brown cloth. There is more than the pale of cold in the captain's white face.

We were upset by a terrible gale off the south cape, he says while the soldiers disembark. For two days we were lost and without sight of the *Sophia*. One of my sailors fell from the yard and broke his back upon the anchor stock. The mainsail was split down the middle. It was a terrible passage.

Chase crowbars his exhausted legs over the gunwale.

When we came upon the mouth of the harbour, I could not see a way through. It is only now that I have seen the pilot Lucas at the heads. He sailed our ship through.

The prisoners of the *Prince Leopold* are put to work without delay. Cuthbertson sends bands of them into the mouth of Gordon's River under constable guard to build lime kilns and dig for mortar. A system of logging gangs is organised. Whaleboats are sent each morning to basins and inlets on the harbour's northern shoreline They return each evening with rafts of Huon pine lugged behind them. Kelly tells Cuthbertson that there is coal on that coastline too, so farmers and miners are sent together to make camps. In a moment of fancy Cuthbertson wonders if Settlement Island will ever be spoken of like Hobarttown.

Cuthbertson keeps a party of the incorrigible prisoners on the island. It would be irresponsible to send them away from close supervision. He also retains the benign paupers who are good for nothing but manual labour. They are put to work sawing Huon pine for Cuthbertson's schooner. It is the end of April when Cuthbertson is drawn to the dissonance of a soldier coming down on one of these old wretches with a crop.

The convict is sobbing when Cuthbertson arrives. He is a

stick of a man, pale except for long patches on his body which are bruised blue. The soldier strikes him again and bleats at him to get up. The convict's knees are in his stomach and his hands are sewn over his head.

The soldier explains that he refuses to work. Cuthbertson orders two constables to lift the man to his feet. His raw ankles and tender soles seem unwilling to stand free so the constables suspend him in the air.

Cuthbertson asks the prisoner his name.

John Ollery. I am tired, tired.

Cuthbertson did not ask him if he was tired.

Put him in the pillory on the beach, Cuthbertson orders the constables. There are a handful of prisoners watching on. It is 50 lashes for disobedience and refusal to work, he says with calm.

The prisoners return to their saws. When Cuthbertson returns to the officers' huts, he asks John Douglas to make a note of 50 lashes for Ollery, to be dispensed on the morrow.

He gives them out at muster. Each morning is the same, except this is the first morning that John Douglas has a name in his black book of convict indictments. It is the first public flogging at Settlement Island.

But there is some hesitation in Douglas's voice as he reminds Cuthbertson of the charge while they wait for the convicts to be arranged on the sandy ground in front of them.

There was word last night that Ollery was broken by the work. This is all Douglas says because Cuthbertson looks so heavy on him that he turns his face down.

Broken by the work? Cuthbertson repeats as he rises to his sandstone pulpit above the morning muster. Idleness, he says to Douglas, looking down. Idleness is a noxious root. You pull the weed out as soon as it takes to the soil. You do not wait for it to flower. You may be sympathetic to those still subject to your former condition, but your sympathy is misplaced. If you allow a man to rest and deny orders, the idea will set in the minds of others. I will not let it set.

Cuthbertson raises his voice to the lines of magpied prisoners which fill the yard beneath him: On this island you are gathered to work, and work for the sake of your sins. This is your last refuge. It is your chance to escape damnation. If you apply yourselves here, you may be deemed worthy to return to the country of civilised persons. If you are not idle, if you are industrious, if you are obedient, if you are productive. Disobedience will not be tolerated.

Cuthbertson motions to the constables who carry John Ollery to the triangle. His eyes are deeply caved. He has no fight in him. The constables remove his shirt without tearing it. Cuthbertson shrugs away his own coat. He exchanges it for the lash. Ollery's back is crossed with the faint alabaster scars of a distant flogging. His soft skin has not felt the lash in some time.

Some of you may think it is possible to escape your work through protest. Cuthbertson raises the lash and plies it hard against Ollery's trembling back. He cannot hear any scream through the tear and crack. He strides fifty paces across the yard then returns, giving the flesh time to rise and blister. After the first strike there are nine angry red marks on the skin. Cuthbertson draws blood on his second. This time he hears the scream.

Ollery's white legs, stained with red runnels, fail him after 25 lashes. Blood pools and bubbles in the sand. His hands are twisted where they are bound. The muster watches as Cuthbertson paces up and down between strikes. He has flogged many men, and each flogging has been patient.

He counts every stroke, and on the thirtieth it seems that the wailing ends. Ollery's body is limp, his wrists a dark purple lump in their stirrups, his hands stretched under the weight of an unconscious body. His back is gored like legs of squid.

Cuthbertson commands a constable near at hand to toss a pail of water over him. The water flushes the wounds. Ollery rises and screams. Cuthbertson goes again. He accomplishes five more before the surgeon James Scott stops him.

The surgeon crouches at the triangle and is quiet. Cuthbertson can hear the cringing of his wounds, pussing and whining as they fatten. Then the surgeon orders the constables to take Ollery down and carry him to the hospital. Cuthbertson returns the fleshy lash to his lackey and regains his coat. He closes buttons over his blood-spattered undershirt. He rises again to the pulpit and takes up the register of occupations from Douglas. Before he begins, his little finger ventures to his eye and scoops some bloody gunk from the duct.

The convicts look mauled by what they have seen. None of them will be wilful today.

Once the muster is complete Cuthbertson cuts a path to the hospital. He finds Scott with his hands on the body of John Ollery. The convict's open eyes are drying fast. There is a grave and obscure look upon the face of the surgeon. Cuthbertson cannot tell if it is pity or disgust.

CUTHBERTSON

Macquarie Harbour, 1822 A.D.

Private Reynolds's face is haggard in the play of the hospital's shadows. He is like a hollow drum which, despite Cuthbertson's knocking, returns only sound without shape.

Reynolds?

The private's mouth opens without words.

Take the prisoner's body in a boat and bury it off the island.

Off the island, sir? Reynolds regards the mass of John Ollery's gored flesh with repugnance.

There is scarcely enough land here for the living. Take it sou'west. There is an island near the cape. Bury it there. Do not mark the grave.

Cuthbertson turns to James Scott and says: He was killed by a visitation of God upon the heart.

Reynolds gathers convict constables to him and makes them wrap the body in cloth. Cuthbertson watches as a whaleboat pushes away from the slipway, bearing the hastily embalmed body of John Ollery across the water to the nameless island in the sou'west.

In a few days Cuthbertson learns from Douglas that the prisoners are speaking of Ollery's murder. Cuthbertson corrects the word murder, but hopes that whatever their opinion, it will keep them in line.

Douglas offends this wish: They are saying Ollery's gone on 'oliday. I've heard it with my ears. They are calling the island where he is buried holiday island.

Even an unmarked grave cannot erase the man's name, sucks Cuthbertson bitterly. He thinks the prisoners foul and crude. The following morning the convicts sing at muster. He cannot flog them all:

Now I am one that never lied to you,

And I never yet took a bribe;

I carry off the youth and the elders,

And the strongest man alive;

I take them with me before the Only Son,

Reading lists of their sins in hand;

And I will take you with me, my fair, sprightly John;

Dispute no more, come along.

He knows the song from Ireland. It is the first time he feels the genuine flutter of uprising. But a fortnight later Cuthbertson's fears are put to bed. A band of prisoners bolt from their labour on the main and disappear into the bush. They flee and do not fight.

When Cuthbertson hears that eight convicts have gone, led by a prisoner named Saunders, he rushes to the jetty. He takes Private Reynolds and another private named Parker and gives them a kangaroo dog each. He arms three reformed convicts to serve them. The dogs are given the sniff of articles particular to the escapees, and the party pushes away in a boat.

Cuthbertson watches them row south until the oars are lost in the curling waves.

None of them return. Not the eight convicts or the three constables or the two dogs or his soldiers. None. It is July and there has not been sight or sound for three months. It is a searing loss, his lieutenant's guard reduced to fifteen. At least if Ollery's death cannot put them off, the dispassionate silence and horror of thirteen missing souls might. And for those who will risk escape, Cuthbertson thinks, he will not waste any more men. Let them discover the hell that lies beyond.

PEARCE

Van Diemen's Land, 1822 A.D.

Atkinson is under the ground now. So far as Pearce knows, Davis and Churton got away. Saunders and the others have been sent to Newcastle on the main – he is sure of that. He has not seen them. But it is he who gets the worst punishment of all: he is sent to join the murderer Cuthbertson at Macquarie Harbour.

When the ship Alexander is bound to join returns from the west, it brings vivid tellings of their secondary prison.

We're going to China, a prisoner named Chevel murmurs in the cells below deck.

He is insulted by a brash ex-soldier named Dalton. You do not know what China is, Chevel. China is a teapot so far as you know.

There is poisonous woods there, says another, and it snows in summer.

Cannot be hell then can it? says Dalton. A place as cold as that.

It isn't heaven. They say you can't escape, says Chevel.

That is what they want you to think. Dalton turns his unctuous voice to something of a whisper. I hear from one of the sailors them boys Green and Saunders, they got out of there in May. I hear Green and Saunders been seen in the midlands.

Saunders? Alexander asks. Joseph Saunders? No one answers him.

When he is allowed on deck Alexander rues the memory of Patrick Hart's scalped head. He once said the prison hulks in Britain were retired warships from the Seven Years' War. It is the flip of the colours in the open air above the yardarm that reminds him. The naval ensign, deep blue with the flag of union in its corner, mocks its Irish prisoners. This is another thing that Hart said: The emblem of England sits heavily upon saint Patrick's cross.

The wind enlivens the flag as though it can hear Alexander think. The fabric looks like it is writhing. The memory goes on: They could not make the old country like the face of that flag, with the Irish below, the dissenting Scots in the midsection and the English in dress circle. So they created a country where the flag could be realised.

The flag apprehends Alexander's eye as bruised and blooded white flesh.

Alexander loses count of days in the dimness of the bilge. A week travels like a month. Most nights he murmurs in the depths of the groaning vessel with the other Irishman, Dalton, a deserter of the army in Gibraltar, a fiery 25 year old with a piebald face.

Alexander can only dream of foreign cities and harbours more colourful than Hobart. He is a man ringed with 32 years of living, whose free life took him the paltry distance from county Monaghan to Cork Harbour – his entire life in 50 miles. He wonders why a man would desert.

Alexander cannot imagine Dalton in a pressed red coat. He is a crude, swearing man who pisses on the ballast around them without a care for its smell. But he is company, and in the darkness they dig at their own wounds and open them up. It is the only means of passing the time in the darkness of the ship's stomach, like tattooing oneself with symbols of the past.

Dalton knows much about Macquarie Harbour. He speaks as confidently about something he knows nothing about as a subject on which he is a scholar. It comforts Alexander. Alexander does not have as much wisdom as he has curiosity, so he soaks in Dalton's words. He cannot sift the truth from the lies.

The commandant there is from the 48th regiment, Dalton narrates. I heard tales of them when I was in the army in Gibraltar. The steelbacks they call them. I never seen a soldier from the 48th but I hear their commanders love the lash more than any other. Half of them cannot even touch their toes with their fingers. The skin of their backs is taut as boiled leather. I hear their privates do not even feel flogging on account of these scars.

Alexander does not tell Dalton that he knows Lieutenant Cuthbertson.

Dalton tells him about his own back, lately flogged. The fucker that flogged me did not know how to flog a man, Dalton says, peeling up his shirt.

Did you ever flog a man in the army? Alexander asks.

Not many. A few.

You would not flog a chum.

Dalton bends a wicked smile. Only if I didn't like him.

Alexander thinks Sarah Island is the most desolate place he has ever seen. It appears in the fog as a black spit on the edge of his sight, suspended in white sky and red water. There are mountains on all sides. In the deep distance, the blanched sky hardens the edges of peaks which retreat forever. They are pyramids of dark dough whose excess has been cut out of the floured board of clouds.

Alexander traps the glancing victory of a single beam of sunlight, escaping the dense clouds a thousand miles away. It glints on the tip of a careening white mountain. Dalton looks with him. He calls it Frenchman's Cap. He says it is named for the conical cap of liberty worn by the French when they overthrew their tyrant king.

Alexander touches the brooch in his pocket. He remembers when he was a child. He thought it was a loaf of bread for so many years, until he learned it was the cap of liberty. He does not recall any of his father's friends wearing conical caps. They only mired their faces. He wonders if that is why they failed.

As they draw nearer to Sarah Island, Alexander can see a

fence climb to the highest part of the island. It is some kind of a windbreak. The fence quivers in the galling ocean wind. Buildings lean on rudimentary brick chimney stacks like crutches. The other shanties and storehouses depict the ghetto of a coal-town. On the southern tip of the island is a naval slipway which cradles the skeleton of a yellow schooner.

A detachment of bodies in discoloured pink coats awaits them on the jetty. Alexander retches when he sees Cuthbertson's straight frame.

His coat is bright red and streaked with white, where the backs of his soldiers are patched and brown. The silver buttons on his breast are polished to a dark gleam, and he wears crossed belts over his chest. His black boots reach his knees, polished also to a dark lick despite the mud on which all men stand. There is a dark leather cap on his head which erupts with a red-white plume. The cap bears a badge of polished brass with the impression *48* on it. There is that strange word: TALAVERA; and on his chest is a golden crescent.

The prisoners are searched. Alexander watches a short man scribble in a damp, foxed book which he labours in vain to shelter from the sea spray. At times Cuthbertson leans close to him and moves his lips. Long, thick silver whiskers reinforce his dark eyes. When Alexander meets his eyes he cannot tell if he is recognised. His gaze is too callous.

Macquarie Harbour spills all around them as they are marched up the hill to their barracks. Alexander can see the mountains better from the hill. He looks again at Frenchman's

Cap in the nor'east, and then along the drawn coastline, which advances and retreats like a black tide. Even in the south there is a wrinkle of green mountains, and beyond that the blue teeth of ranges, and further still serried grey towers white with clouds and snow. Alexander does not know how any man can escape.

This night, as Alexander secures his hammock to a post, he is arrested by the unsettling familiarity of a voice.

Jesus Christ. It cannot be Polly Pearce.

Alexander turns and fills his eyes with the ghost of Tom Lawton. Letting stands with him. Alexander looks for Saunders. He does not know if he feels joy or fear. Letting's scowl worsens.

How did you end up here? he asks in a voice fatigued by hatred.

I thought you were gone to Newcastle, says Alexander.

Lawton laughs and draws closer. He takes Alexander's shoulders in his arm. It is good to see you, Polly, he says. I thought you'd be living large after your pardon, married to that blowsy slut Alice Kelley.

What pardon? askes Alexander.

Lawton's arm tenses around his neck. What pardon indeed, you fetching—

Alexander kicks and struggles in his grip.

Where's Atkinson? Letting howls. Lawton doubles Alexander over and Letting kicks him in the face. Viscid gouts of blood hang out of his nose. Alexander shuts his eyes against the second kick, but Dalton rushes Letting and puts him on the ground before it lands.

I will hide you, he warns. Lawton loosens his arm.

Alexander's face is hot with blood. Atkinson is dead, he cries, blood falling in his mouth. There was a hundred pounds on his head.

Did you take that money, Polly? Letting sneers.

Cuthbertson hates us all, Alexander snivels.

Good thing for you Saunders is dead, says Lawton. He'd kill you if he weren't.

Alexander stops the bleeding with his sleeve. Saunders is dead?

Escaped. Old boy is having a better time than we, no matter where he is, says Lawton. He pats Letting's shoulder and they walk away.

Alexander tells Dalton the story as they row their logging boat the following morning, but he is interrupted by the voice of the constable who says he will recommend 50 lashes if they are not quiet. So they whisper in the flea-bitten night and draw close together over a meagre fire in the crowded, stinking penitentiary. Each day, as they beat scuds of burgundy water with their oars, Alexander wonders if Saunders is dead or alive.

The work is worse than the road-gang ever was. They are given ration in the morning and nothing to fill their yawning stomachs until dark. After muster they row to Kelly's Basin and cut down the straightest Huon trees, often up to their necks in water so frigid it strangles breath. They lash the wood in rafts and drag them back to the island, wasted arms heaving and thrusting the heavy oars in strokes a fraction of the distance and speed they could draw in the morning. All this to dress the naked ribs of Cuthbertson's prized schooner.

As they wade in the water, away from the dry overseer, Dalton and Alexander get to talking with another prisoner named Bill Kennerly. He tells them that Green and Saunders are alive.

Two redcoats went after them with prisoners and kangaroo dogs, debates Alexander. All armed, I hear. And none came back. How can six unarmed fellers have better fair than soldiers with dogs?

You said it yourself Alexander, goes Kennerly. They was all armed. *I heard* the convicts and the redcoats sent by the commandant broke out in a brawl when they landed. *I heard* the redcoats were killed and the constables followed the other eight. Wouldn't you? Kennerly defends the principle that their disappearance does not mean their death.

The daily punishments increase because of this thinking. Men are beaten more frequently and without being recorded in the clerk's soggy book. One of these is an Irish butcher in Alexander's logging gang named Matthew Travers. When Cuthbertson reads the charge, it is for: Conniving to escape. Twenty-five lashes.

Mad Jack stands above the convicts at morning muster, his cottage nudged against the hillside behind him. As he reads the charges, Alexander cannot find Dalton. When the butcher is stripped and tied to the triangle, Alexander sees Dalton called forth by the constables, a cat o' nine tails in his hand. Dalton is still flogging the butcher Travers when Alexander is jostled away to the jetty.

He pretends not to know Dalton after this, and he is glad that he does, because the man at the oars beside him the following morning is named Greenhill. He is Travers's mate. It takes Alexander a while to square it, an Irish butcher like Travers close-knit with a man like Bob Greenhill, an Englishman. Alexander supposes birth cribs mean little in a place like Macquarie Harbour. In their world there is only convict and free; and among the convicts there is traitor and friend. Constable Loggins, who sits in the bow of their whaleboat, fingering his cudgel, he is a traitor. A convict constable. A traitor of kind. Folk like Dalton, the kind that relish flogging other convicts, they are traitors too.

Greenhill calls them traitors of liberty. As he speaks, Alexander relaxes one arm from his oar and slips it free of his jacket. He bares his tattoo, a deep blue-black stain of *D L* encircled by dots. Greenhill's eyes shine with approval. The tattoo is something of a watchword. It grants Alexander entry into the conspiracies of Greenhill's mind.

Greenhill and Alexander whisper in between the strides of the oars. Greenhill flames with hatred for any convict who flogs his common man. But he also flames with hatred for the common man as well.

He calls all the convicts but himself feeble, especially Ollery who is on holiday for 35 lashes. He tells Alexander about his attempted escape from Hobart with Travers and several others the year before, when they stole a schooner on the Derwent River. He says they were caught by government vessels and handed 150 lashes on their backs.

Whatever man dies after 30 is not a man, claims Greenhill in his baritone throat. He says he and Travers tried to bolt again even after 150 lashes, but being weak from the flogging they were run down and told that they would be sent to Sarah Island to see out their sentences. They only gave us a Botany Bay dozen after that, he says with no shade of a smile.

Alexander does not know what a Botany Bay dozen is.

That is 25 lashes, says Greenhill. Another hundred might have killed me, but only another hundred.

Is it easy, Alexander asks, to escape by boat?

If you don't get caught. Greenhill eyes Loggins at the aft of the whaler. I been thinking on it a while.

Greenhill leaves Alexander with his own thoughts now. Alexander wonders if the sea turns men mad. Greenhill is a mariner, and from the hour of their meeting Alexander does not know him as anything but aggravated. He mutters to himself and scowls at any person that loans him as little as a wayward eye.

He is ever dishevelled. His dark walnut hair, which sprouts in thick flanks about his jaw, is parched and unkempt. It looks always as if it has been swept up in a squall. If there is some madness inside him it has coloured his outside. Alexander wonders if the sea has done this to him.

One night a few days later, as they stab at their rations,

Greenhill again tells the story of his failed escape with Travers.

Matt Travers sits beside him in quiet contemplation, his face hurt by the tale. He is still recovering from the open sores on his back, which the surgeon lathered with pig's fat before sending him back to work. They are Dalton's sores.

We would have made it, Greenhill says. Travers concurs. If it weren't for those bastards what held us back. They said we laid our legs on our necks and they jumped ship. Cowards.

There is something in Greenhill's eye that makes Alexander believe he has not abandoned the hope of sailing out of Van Diemen's Land.

CUTHBERTSON

Macquarie Harbour, 1822 A.D.

In the weeks that follow the escape, the rumours that all have perished are enough to flatten the convicts. But Cuthbertson knows this will pass. Eventually the whispers of failure become rumours of success, and Douglas tells Cuthbertson some prisoners believe the absconders actually made it through.

That is why Cuthbertson has ordered a train of signal fires to be erected along the coast to alert the island to any escapes. In the event of an attempt by sea, the fires will urge the pilot Lucas to seal the mouth at hell's gates, and draw forth from the island a party in pursuit. The system must be working, thinks Cuthbertson, for although the convicts moan, there has not been another escape since he lost his two soldiers.

What of my *soldiers*? thinks Cuthbertson, despairing that 17 has become 15 − yet the convict numbers only grow. The officials and justices insist on sending shiploads upon shiploads of convicts without notice. Cuthbertson makes the best of this horrible burden by putting them to work on the *Governor Sorell*, and in a matter of weeks the schooner is complete. He can hardly believe the rude hands of convicts have built her. She must hold thousands of pounds on the market, and to think Cuthbertson has come by her for free. But even this thought does not comfort him on the day that another ship with 50 years in collected sentences brings Alexander Pearce to his island.

Alexander Pearce. Cuthbertson wishes he did not know his name to look at his face. He looks more haggard than Cuthbertson remembers. His thinning muddle of hair, his sharp upturned nose, his devilish, deep-set hazel eyes. Beside his name on the page of the inward log writhes the word *catholic*.

Sorell had promised to send a religious instructor to the settlement, but Cuthbertson doubts he will ever receive Hobart's unflattering Phillip Conolly. Religious instruction would be useless at Settlement Island anyway. For a wretch like Pearce there is no salvation. In him is bundled all the warts of Ireland.

He loathes sharing nativity with the likes of Alexander Pearce. The common bond reminds him of the cavity he crawled out of. He assures himself that although there was little to separate them in the cot, here at the ends of the Earth they are vastly different men.

What is that boat? Cuthbertson asks Douglas one morning as he surveils the quiet harbour.

Loggins is taking a prisoner to the small island for solitary, sir, Douglas reports with pinched eyes.

Cuthbertson recalls some charges of conspiracy to escape which he has punished variously with the lash and with solitary. It is his hope that those shipped to the small island will distil without the company of other men.

What do you think refines a man more, Douglas, the lash or solitary?

Do you mean refine or break, sir?

Cuthbertson shrugs. Sometimes you have to break a bone for it to heal straight. Mind or the body—which doorway is open to reformation?

Douglas looks up from his task and seems to cast his eye over the whole island. He speaks: The prisoners of good conduct that came here with us, what is it that makes them good?

This is your question to answer, Cuthbertson insists.

I will say this, sir, Douglas remarks after a drawn thought. I have seen some men lashed who, on the end of a canary, do not suffer a sound. I have seen other men punished with 25 and cry out at the second strike, and keep crying before the end.

Cuthbertson thinks of John Ollery.

On the former, I cannot tell if it is their mind or their body that carries them through in silence. Maybe it is a divorce of the two. On that very point the same hard man can be isolated for a month and come out crazed, where the man weak of body remains himself.

When I was a private, Cuthbertson speaks, I saw men go mad after the battle was done. The cannon would rip a man's limbs off, so indiscriminate that it was like God rolling a die.

Some boys that lost limbs, those who survived and were sent back home, I saw some of them in Ireland before coming here, and though bastardised by the world after losing their hand or foot, they were much the same, still telling the same jokes or swearing in line with their character. The boys who missed a maiming, the ones that *watched* the cannonballs knock off those limbs, it didn't matter what company they were in during the war, they lived in the company of madness after that. They held a musket shaky, and their eyes began to wander. It is no wonder most of my comrades that went like that never made it through. They took sick and didn't have the will to fight it, or they got blown up themselves.

You ask about the good prisoners. I reckon they were always good. Corrupted in the eyes of the law, for certain, but show them the error of their ways and see how soon they lick authority's boots. But some of the men sent here … there is no refining them, and there never was. True, lashing a hard man makes him harder, but the cat is our only authority in this hellish colony.

How to reform a man? I'd say the man reforms himself. Whip a repentant man and he will cry out for fear of another flogging. Place him on the small island and his mind will soften. But whip a recalcitrant and he will hate you for it; put a hard mind through hell and the fire will only harden it further. That is why this colony needs its own supreme court, because convicts like that Pearce, mark my words, they're good for nothing more than hard labour and six feet of rope.

You need the lash to stay on top. That is what this post has taught me. For the softer ones will always fall into line, but the hard ones, throw them in a pit and they'll eat each other. That is why convict constables are so diligent.

So is there no hope for the souls of all men?

Cuthbertson watches the faint boat arrive at the small island. This business has nothing to do with repentance, Cuthbertson says. These wretches are past that. When each new boat arrives, they do not see purgatory's gates at the heads of Macquarie Harbour. This is no waiting place. This is final. Those are hell's gates over yonder.

Cuthbertson does not linger to discuss the conditions of his statement, like the reluctance of the convicts to accept hell's gates as their final threshold. He walks to the slipway to spend time with his schooner. He cares to keep sand from spoiling the tops of his boots and climbs to the high aft of his prize. He looks out over the harbour to the infernal bush which a convict would be mad to try and defeat. Something glinting and small flickers in the corner of his eye.

He looks into the north. At first it is a lonely candle on the verge of the maroon horizon, but then another sparks beside it. In a passage of moments an eerie train of lights comes into the world, growing brighter and more ominous like wisp lights in the bog.

PEARCE

Macquarie Harbour, 1822 A.D.

Alexander did not think he had fat on his arms to lose when he departed Hobart, but each morning his veins burgeon like earthworms, a new rib presses against the skin of his shrunken gut, his wrists waste, and the face in the dirty, borrowed looking glass seems gaunter.

Alexander lies awake at night and wonders what shape his life would have taken had he kept communion with Patrick Hart. He thinks of the twisted face of Jesus Christ on a white wall and the smell of tar. Was he safer in that company? Dalton is like Hart, who makes use of rebellious words to kindle warmth, but they are nothing more than words. He is not strong enough to fight the soldiers, even if he was in the army. It is Saunders he should have stayed away from, it is Saunders who brought him here. Alexander got Hart and Saunders the wrong way around – but he does not know what to do about Dalton.

Every night they speak of escape across the fire. This night, in the amber handle of the flames, Greenhill takes a crooked needle and gives himself and Travers the likeness of Alexander's *Death or Liberty* tattoo. Alexander thinks it makes him one of them.

It's all a lie they tell us to keep us low, Greenhill says of Saunders.

I never heard a sailor speak so highly of inland travel, Chevel snivels. What you going to do without a compass, eh? How the hell you going to find your way when you can't see thro' the trees?

You're a bastard, Chevel, Greenhill says. He falls quiet and turns in on himself. Alexander lies near them. They are whispering. Alexander feels the formwork of their plan.

You notice they don't give Loggins a gun, Greenhill says. Wouldn't be hard to put him down and take the whaler. Sail it to hell's gates. Lucas is often away from the heads, running errands to the island. His station will be full of stores. Greenhill rubs his hands together.

How come no one has tried it? Alexander asks.

Can you box a compass? Greenhill flares. I can navigate my way on a barren sea. I've been a mariner all my life. We could make it.

To where? Alexander asks.

Anywhere. China. Valdivia. After that, who knows? Anywhere but New South Wales.

How many do we need?

Eight. Eight to the oars.

Alexander feels the catch of Travers's eye. Eh, you, says the butcher. You're mates with that flogger.

Alexander mumbles, I am not mates with no flogger.

You fucking are.

Alexander prays that Dalton will remain on the other side of the big fire. If he comes into their light and calls Alexander by name, Alexander knows his tattoo will not save him from Travers's hatred.

He has seldom spoken with Dalton since the day that he flogged Travers on Mad Jack Robertson's order. When he had next seen him he had asked on desperate enquiring breath, Why in hell did you do it?

Dalton's only reply was cool and disheartening: The soldiers knew I was in the army so they asked if I would not do it for a pinch of tobacco. Could be I get into the constabulary. Yea, better to have the commandant's favour, yea. Better flog than be flogged, really. Could be I share what I get, when Cuthbertson rewards me with rations. Keep close now, Pearce.

He's mates with that flogger Dalton, Travers says again to Greenhill. I don't want them in any part of this.

We need eight pairs of arms, Greenhill asserts. He does not raise his dark eyes from Alexander. We've not much choice in that. Eh Pearce, you mates with that flogger?

I knew him on the boat, Bob, that was all. You fellers know what 'tis like.

Bet your breech I know what 'tis like. Just wait till that bastard flogs you, Travers sneers.

Greenhill settles his mate. He doesn't vouch for Alexander but he doesn't condemn him either. He carries on with his plan. They will bide their time until Lucas's next visit to Sarah Island, putting aside tinder and what other wherewithal they can muster for a sea voyage. When the day is upon them they will knock out Constable Loggins, take the whaleboat and row along the coast to hell's gates. There they will be free to the liberty of the open sea.

In the coming days, Kennerly and Dalton become permanent bodies in their fireside conspiracy. Travers seethes in silence and shames Alexander with accusing eyes. Greenhill says again: We need eight pairs of arms. The plan is then sealed when three more prisoners are appointed to their logging gang. Greenhill retraces his scheme like old ground, careful to keep his words within their company of eight.

The day of Lucas's absence arrives, but at morning muster Greenhill's name is called among the coal miners and not the logging gang. The stare which he gives Travers and Alexander is lasting and insistent.

They have caught wind of us, Alexander says to Travers as they row.

Don't be a coward. You don't know that. Travers is adamant. It doesn't matter. We can get Bob from the mines. I saw his look as he walked away this morning. He will expect us.

The sea is whipped into sanguine froth. At Kelly's Basin the gang marks a stand of straight pines as though it is ordinary business. Loggins is watching Kennerly closely when Travers comes behind him with a branch in hand. Loggins must understand some urgency in Alexander's nervous eyes, but he turns too late.

Travers clubs him across the face and the overseer falls into the mud. What happens now happens quickly.

Travers jumps on Loggins's body and cries for help. He strips the man bare. Alexander and Kennerly tie him to a tree and gag him.

We should cut off his ballocks, Dalton proposes, glaring at the overseer's naked flesh.

Travers ignores him.

We should kill him, Dalton opines.

Do that and we are dead men if caught, Kennerly decrees.

Faith, says Dalton. Better than Macquarie Harbour.

Alexander does not think Dalton truly means that.

Travers runs away to the whaler, calling back at Dalton on his strides: If you would rather die, stay here and wait for the redcoats.

Alexander runs behind Travers and Dalton chases after.

They all push the boat into the water and jump inside. There are three hatchets with them from the logging camp. Travers keeps one spread across his lap, and the other two are with Kennerly and a man called Bodenham. In the rush, Alexander had not thought to grasp one.

For the first time in days Alexander feels the heat in his blood. Steam whispers on his blue veins. It is briefly exhausted by the feeling that he cannot trust Greenhill. But he has no choice. A flea does not discriminate over the rat it ought to ride when rats are running the distance. Alexander tries to dismiss the thought of being trapped in an empty sea with Travers and Dalton trying to kill one another.

He looks sou'west to Sarah Island, rising like a whale's back beyond the waves. Travers says the pricks cannot see them.

Together they beat the waves in silence, muted by the weight of their gamble. Then Dalton speaks: We should have cut off his balls.

I have had too much of you, flogger, Travers warns. There is more at stake than Loggins's ballocks. Travers peers sou'west to the island even as he speaks. Dalton looks at Alexander and sullies him with a wink.

They reach the promontory of Coal Head in a couple of hours and Farm Cove soon after that. Alexander can see the shape of Greenhill's body on the distant shore. Greenhill dashes into the water, jacket open. He calls some of them to follow him to the beach.

They beach the whaler down the strand from a bark hut. Travers remains with the boat. Greenhill starts towards the miner's humpy. He breaks down the door. Inside they grasp sacks of flour and racks of beef white with salt. Garlic hangs from the ceiling. There is the clutter of adzes, picks and shovels. The fireplace smoulders. Greenhill shoulders kangaroo coats and orders each man to take one. Alexander dresses himself in meat, and as he does, he sees a hefty broad axe leaning in the door. He strides towards it and stretches out his arm but Greenhill takes it first. The sailor's eye is strange and he clutches it close.

Come on, boys, let's be going before they catch wind of us. Greenhill is the fourth man with an axe now.

We ought to douse the signals, one of the others, named Mather, says outside.

Greenhill lowers his sacks but keeps the axe firm in hand. He consents and altogether they search for pails to dampen the tawny signal beacons.

Satisfied that the signals are wet, they pile into the whaler and beat away from the shore. Greenhill reminds them that they will row north along the coast to the mouth of King's River then slip through hell's gates under darkness. They can overwhelm the sailors at the pilot's station. Even if a ribbon of smoke or flare of fire reaches the commandant then, it will be too late. They will be free.

The men begin to pulse with jubilation. They curse their gaolers, curse the colony. Greenhill tells them they can make it to the islands of the Pacific. There is spice and sex and sun ahead. No more bitter rain and rations. No more meagre meals and that sadist Cuthbertson. All these things are painfully dashed with the sight of a yellow light behind them. Alexander's eye is dragged unwillingly back to Coal Head where a fire is gaining.

Greenhill rushes to the stern. One light is now many. Greenhill nearly rocks the boat to doom in his anger.

Alexander does not know if they have missed a beacon, or if

the miners, privy to their desertion, kindled something else. It does not matter now.

We're damned now. Greenhill looks north over the folding waves. He repeats the curse: We're damned. We're damned. We're damned.

Row north, row north still, says the oldest of them whose name is Brown. We can make it.

Greenhill eyes him with contempt. They've schooners faster than this. Besides, we won't make the gates before nightfall.

The men begin to argue. The boat ceases in the futility of their wrestling. The waves spin it in its place.

Greenhill stands among them and attends their eyes to the mouth of a small creek away to their right. They row there and the whaler is beached.

There is no way by sea now, Greenhill panics. He stands in the middle of the ring of prisoners. Alexander notices him hold his broad axe like a sceptre.

They will be coming up from Coal Head now, the mariner says. Mad Jack will cut us off at the pilot's station if we go any further. We should leave the boat.

They argue over this, but Travers agrees. He says there is no path but land.

We won't make it through, Mather caws.

Horseshit, Travers says. What about Saunders?

He is fucking dead, Dalton scorns. It is the first genuine fright Alexander has heard from him.

Greenhill ends their argument: There is eight of us and we

have food. We're breaking up the boat. They'll not see where we landed.

Greenhill takes his axe to the Huon strakes. He is joined by Travers and then Kennerly and Bodenham. Alexander and Mather carry away the broken jetsam and hide it in the bush.

Now let's be off, Greenhill announces, huffing. He holds the axe in the direction of a double peak that rises above them. We'll make it through lads, don't you worry. Now let's be off. They'll be here soon.

PEARCE

Van Diemen's Land, 1822 A.D.

The island seems larger from above. They clamber hand over foot across the stark face of the mountain, the two spurs of which can be seen from the penitentiary. Alexander recalls looking up at the mountain from the convict barracks. Now he wonders if any of the other prisoners can see them, like ants on the face of a desolate stone.

Alexander knows he is too far away to discern the movement of bodies on Sarah Island, but his eyes believe in moving people. He thinks soldiers, constables, perhaps even Mad Jack himself, hasten after them. Greenhill tells him he is mad, but even Greenhill is reluctant to stop until the sun has gone down.

They light a small fire at night. It is only now, as darkness falls and the firelight hurries in encouraged, golden gouts, that the anxiety of their escape dries away. Alexander cannot fight what feels like a final, due release. They all agree that they have beaten the bastards. Liberty or death. And they have taken liberty.

Their jubilation is cooled by a rising frigid wind that brings westerly rain. They lift their kangaroo skin coats to protect the meek fire and its brittle coals. But they have endured worse than this. For the first time Alexander sees a smile upon Greenhill's face.

I stole a coat in England, Greenhill says once the rain has petered. He gains the ears of the others with the story of his transportation. As he speaks Travers laughs.

Go on, Bob, he says, tell them who charged you.

Greenhill's eyes are dark. Judith. My wife.

His wife, Travers sings with Irish laughter. His own fucking wife charged him with larceny.

She was a right bitch. Said I'd been away at sea too long. She wondered why I stayed away … She were always poorly when I were at home. She cried to the neighbours that I were away, but those same neighbours told me she took some bla'guard in our bed and were always smiling when she was s'posed to be crying over my absence. Bitch said I stole her coat. Everything she owned I paid for. How could I steal what she bought with my money? Court awarded her and gave me 14 years. Greenhill drops beef into his mouth.

Travers's royal laughter falls silent as Dalton begins to speak. He makes a poor choice of story, Alexander thinks, telling how his back was shorn off by flogging for deserting from the army.

The light in Travers's eyes says enough. Alexander glances at Greenhill whose smile has also vanished. Alexander becomes presently aware of how close he is sitting to Dalton.

He knows the others believe the flogger is his mate. The journey will be long, he thinks, feeling the sudden cold, longer than Greenhill suggests. They have meat and flour, but Alexander doubts it is enough to satisfy eight men. Here on this lonely mountain Greenhill is their commandant; he decides who gets what. Alexander feels he should be seated on the other side of the fire, if indeed Greenhill hates Dalton as the lowest among them. They needed the eighth hand for the oars, but now the sea is behind them and more men means more mouths. Yea, better to have the commandant's favour, yea. Alexander recalls Dalton smiling like a fool. He thinks of his words: Keep close now, Pearce.

At morning they cast off a terrible dew that has settled on them overnight. With the victuals evenly distributed, they cut a track over the ridge.

Greenhill goes in front, followed by Travers. Then comes Mather the Scot, Alexander and Dalton in the middle, and Bodenham and Kennerly at the rear. Brown is far behind them, a tall, winnowed husk of a man, long in the bones but weak. He is the slowest of them all.

The length of the second day carries them through mountain snow. Alexander holds to the hope that Greenhill can read country as well as he can read water. The dawn sun shows them east, which is where they walk, but the only other things Alexander knows about this wilderness is Gordon's River, which Greenhill claims to spy far away in the south, and the wanhope of Frenchman's Cap. Beyond this river and this mountain there is nothing else they know.

The mountain falls away into a gully. Their climb at the far side is exhausting. With the tangerine sun split into fingers between the myrtle beeches, they lay out to sleep. At dawn the next day the party is vigorous, but their descent from the mountain plains brings them into a dense fabric of dark and sprawling jungle. Hidden thorns slash their shins – the first of these cuts makes Alexander faint. Their ankles are shaved by the hard heels of their shoes. Alexander can taste water in the air. The ground is as sodden as the bogs of Kelly's Basin, overshadowed by ferns grown close together – all the light is green because of this. The trees close easy paths in tight bonding branches, and as with the lost harbour, the waters of the swamp run red.

At times Alexander cannot see the sky, and when he can, it is a pale blanket with no sun. Greenhill leads them through a forest so verdant it is sickening. Pearce wonders if he knows which way is east.

Brown fails. He has been at their rear since the very beginning, always quiet, always slow. As they wind their way through the sultry dell, Alexander has a mind to turn and look behind him. As he twists, the fellows behind him follow his gaze. Then Greenhill stops in the front. He pauses and cooees. Only his echo replies. Then, at a great distance in the midst of the green bush, the tangled branches part. Brown pushes between them. He raises a weak hand. Greenhill waits for him to catch.

We're all tired, Brown, but if you fall behind you'll be left. Do you understand?

Brown says nothing, just leans on his haunches and huffs. Greenhill rearranges his broad axe and carries on. Only darkness stops them. They have not made it free of the woods.

The whole world is wet, though Travers manages to light a fire. They mix flour with the swamp water to cook damper, but Alexander cannot keep the damper down.

There is doubt as to where they have wandered. Greenhill rejects the claim that their travail is aimless. He shouts down the other men of the band. He says they will die without him. He says he knows where Gordon's River is but that they should keep clear of it to avoid the soldiers. Alexander doubts any soldiers are coming.

The rain continues this night. When it passes, the weather turns to a foul and foggy breath which hides everything that hurts their feet. The fourth day is no better and they talk little. On the first day their silence had been for fear – now they do not speak to conserve their willpower.

Dalton whispers to Alexander as they walk. The rattling pots weigh more than they should. He says of Greenhill: He is going to lead us to our death.

Alexander ignores him.

They make their way in a long teased line like the tortured thread of an old garment halfway up a barren hill. Night arrests them here. This time Travers cannot light the fire. He bleeds his hands trying. The situation is worsened when Greenhill looks over the provisions and says nothing. When he is asked he says: Perhaps we ought to leave this night and save what's left for tomorrow.

Kennerly cries and stamps. He calls himself a wretch for following Greenhill. He says he should have stayed at Sarah Island where he could at least eat at night.

Bodenham backs him up, shouting: We won't walk out 'is country wiv' our lives. Least wiv' our minds.

Greenhill, who is ever one to bite back when abused, goes quiet. This troubles Alexander more than anything. Greenhill raises his eyes to Travers, glancing as though in signals their years of bondage have taught them. Kennerly gives up and disappears in the direction of Dalton and Brown. Bodenham follows. They are all quite separate now.

Alexander stays with Greenhill and Travers. From very far he catches the occasional shifts of Dalton's eyes. His look is plaintive.

The rain does not cease on the fifth day – is it the fifth day? Already the soles of Alexander's shoes have fallen away. He has noticed in the fleeting light of the moon the raw bottoms of his feet. He can scarcely feel them in the cold.

Torrents sweep across them as they climb. Baskets of needles. They take the next day in rest, whichever day this is. Their kangaroo coats are torn into strips but the leather tastes like hobble straps even though it is boiled.

Alexander's stomach has disappeared. The stinging has collapsed in on itself. It has become a pain that starts at his smallest bowel and reaches his throat. He lies on his side to abate it and stares into the pale sky.

Dalton crawls across to him one day.

What you been saying ... Greenhill? His brindle face is caved with hunger. Alexander does not answer him. Breathing is a task. Dalton summons a breath: Pearce, why you gone away?

Alexander can think but he cannot speak: I am not going anywhere. We are not going anywhere.

Dalton begins to cry and Alexander wonders where he finds the tears. Blood is thicker than water, Alexander thinks, and thicker than tears. Alexander has not been mangled on the triangles with Dalton. Greenhill and Travers have been mangled together. That is why they are mates – their blood is one blood. Alexander and Dalton are not mates. They are nothing at all.

The hours slip away.

Kennerly. Get wood for fire. This is Greenhill's voice.

My arse. Stick it up yours. This is Kennerly's voice.

I'll cut your head open. Greenhill still has the axe.

Kennerly is gone.

Which day is it? Sundays do not matter. They rest most days now. Alexander has a claw on his belly all the time. It is attached to his navel.

Kennerly comes back. He does have wood in his arms. Alexander does not know how he has the strength to carry it.

So hungry, he says. I could eat a piece of a man.

It is not the words that chill Alexander but the look in Greenhill's eye.

It is the next day when Alexander finds himself together with Greenhill, Travers and Mather. Where are the others? Far behind.

What make you of Kennerly? This is Travers talking.

Mather calls it: Flesh of man nonsense.

Pious, you are. Alexander looks at Greenhill. Believes there is venom in the corners of his mouth. Piety prays for rain, survival digs a well, Greenhill says.

Alexander agrees but says nothing. Greenhill goes on: I seen it done before.

Alexander does not know entirely what he means.

Mather has a look on his face.

Greenhill tells a story. Alexander loses half of it. He does not care for a story this instant.

We was weeks off India. No sign of port or hope. Everything gone to pot. A young boy on the ship take ill. He was going to die anyway.

There is enough silence afterwards that Alexander understands.

Greenhill tells them that human flesh tastes like pork. Mather reviles. Greenhill calls him pious again. Says he never tried it, only heard about the pork. Mather says would be murder to do it.

Greenhill puts two things beside one another: murder or death. Asks Mather to choose. Travers puts up two more things: liberty or death.

Greenhill: I will eat the first part. Need you lend a hand in the guilt of it.

Mather: Devil speaks in you. Murder.

Greenhill: We all killed. Any different?

Alexander to himself: I have not.

Mather – Alexander notices no Travers yet: God will never forgive. Going to hell.

Finally, Travers: Been to hell. Any different?

Mather again: I will have a hand in my own condemnation.

Mather surprisingly lucid. Greenhill plays a trick.

Greenhill: Bloody right. We all have a hand in it. There, our burden is lighter.

Alexander hates this next word.

Pearce?

It is Greenhill asking.

His heart beats like it is failing. If he does it, there is nothing after. If he does not, there is nothing after. Which nothingness do you want? To be full of nothingness or void of anything? Alexander? Pearce?

Greenhill: Pearce?

Alexander: I cannot go hungry.

Somehow things are clearer now. Alexander's mouth is wet for the first time in many days. Mather is a combination of tortured parts. He speaks.

How can we pass judgement on one of them?

Greenhill is quick to reply: Mad Jack stood on his pulpit and flogged Ollery dead. What god gave him the authority to do that? If it's the same one what crowned King George, the same king whose law brought us here, then I couldn't give a damn about whether or not we are fit to pass judgement. I think we're better suited to judge our fellows than any cur in a red coat or a white wig.

Surprisingly lucid.

Who should it be? Travers asks.

Alexander looks at the broad axe and wonders if Greenhill had thought about this even before Kennerly uttered piece of man.

Dalton.

Alexander swallows. It hurts.

Greenhill says secondly, Dead men tell no tales.

Mather says, God, again.

Greenhill says, It is decided.

Alexander sees Greenhill and Travers's faces larger than they are. The good fortune of a navigator has expired. Alexander wonders if God or the devil put a butcher in their company.

At night Dalton and others lay away. Behind a windbreak. Alexander does not sleep. Watches Greenhill. Greenhill does not sleep. Makes double sure in his mind they said Dalton not Pearce. Decides Dalton.

It is not morning and not night. Greenhill gets up. Travers and Mather get up. Alexander gets up.

Greenhill carries axe in hand. It is above his head. Silence. Drops—sound. Silence.

Alexander's eyes adjust. Now his ears are filled with screaming.

Christ!

Fuck!

Much scrambling. Dalton says nothing. Scream not his. Very loud sound is Travers taking knife to Dalton's throat. Dalton is now upside down on Greenhill and Mather. They empty him. The others are gone, but not vanished, distant. Shadows in the deep shadowless night. Smirk of moon.

Knife again, clothes torn off. Distinct and sour taste of water on tongue. Bad taste. Is it guilt?

Fire stoked up. Dalton looks nothing like Dalton now. Fire very hot. Travers's hands filthy. Something on the flames.

Day. The others have gone. Dead men tell no tales, but living ones do. If they get back they will make the murderers wanted men for eternity. Alexander feels a tide reaching up to him – he has eaten up the nothingness and now there is nothing to look forward to.

He wonders if it is better than being dead. He is too tired to think of these things – so he walks on, into the tidal nothingness of yellow grass.

ACT THREE

CONOLLY

Hobart-town, 1823 A.D.

The news rips through the settlement like an illness: Governor Sorell is being recalled. It is no secret that Mis'ess Sorell is in fact Mis'ess Kent. It has now become apparent that Mister Kent was never appeased with being cuckolded. To the colonists, the fact does not matter – even Phillip has come to terms with it – they feel it makes him one of them. Sorell is a generous man, a stern politician, and he is living with another man's wife. But his employers take issue with the slander and it has caught up with him at last.

Phillip hears by the bye that the true Mis'ess Sorell and Mister Kent have lit such a fire in London that the government can no longer tolerate Sorell in high office. Phillip is not happy about it. He likes Sorell, even if it is for the simple vain reason that he was gracious to the colony's first catholic priest when he did not have to be. Then again, Phillip expects Sorell understood then the value in a man who can smooth the ruffled feathers of catholics in a country where Irish is not spoken and home is far away. But although Phillip was given grace to be a peacemaker, he is not so cynical that he cannot thank Sorell for kindness.

This opinion is sured up at Sorell's eleventh hour when he gives Phillip one more gift: he gives him five acres of land.

To build a church, says the waning governor.

Phillip has never owned land in his life. Technically he does not own the governor's gift. It is the property of the catholic church, for the purpose of religious observance. But at least it will give Phillip a place to live, segregated from the reprobates of Hobart-town.

Why did you stay with Mis'ess Kent? Phillip asks the governor one day in September.

Because I love her, and love conquers all, Sorell says in their quiet audience in derelict government house. Sorell has moved out of Birch House, for guilt, Phillip thinks.

Love is the most destructive force that God created, Phillip speaks absently, uncommitted to the phrase.

How can you say that, the governor asks, with what Phillip perceives as genuine concern, when you are surrounded by such debased characters - excess, violence and poverty? I do not believe you. Perhaps you have not loved another.

It is not my commission.

The Lord teaches us to love.

Phillip wonders if the governor is trying to excuse his adultery. Sorell is reclined on a sofa, one foot upon the ground, his right leg stretched on cushions. His jacket is off. His casual charm is the source of all his adoration, Phillip thinks. He wonders in this moment if the forthcoming governor, a man named George Arthur, will inspire the same affection.

When are you taking your leave?

Not until March of next year. Worry not, reverend, you have me a while longer yet. He leans forward and pats Phillip on the knee. We are cut of the same cloth, Arthur and I. He was raised on the army's bosom. We are soldiers from circumcision, as it were.

Phillip is told nothing else of the man. He leaves government house with the unsettling apparition of foreskin in his mind.

In the days that follow, Phillip's church comes to bear. He has never built a building either, and after a few weeks, when the skeleton of the church is completed, the grant begins to wane. The roof is shingled, the walls boarded, but the wind blows through it. The money runs out. The floorboards bow. The ceiling is rafters, already with the spit of sparrow droppings and mud of their nests. The grant has gotten as far as dressing the building but no further to fill it with soul.

The altar is fleeced, the pews barren. It feels hard and cold to Phillip, a high and sighing building, full of air and uncertain of ghost. No matter the floods of light its windows and cracks drink in, the place never glows. The first service is draughty, little better than a goods store – the salient difference is the lack of food for mice to hide in.

Phillip sits on the front stair and looks down on the town of

Hobart on the first Sunday of St Virgil's church.

Who was saint Virgil? Sophia Nightingale asks him as they sit together watching Mary Ann pick yellow flowers.

It is not yet consecrated with that name, Phillip says softly, ignoring the question. Phillip has blessed it, but churches take weeks to be consecrated. I should not be holding mass, he adds, but I could not conduct another service down there, in bond stores and wool stores and every other damp cranny that catholics are driven into in the absence of their own church.

Would you not marry two people, then, reverend? Sophia asks.

Marriage is on the nose in this colony, Phillip says. Even the governor has saved on the wedding and chosen another man's wife.

Sophia looks on him with the softness of down. You are so grave, she teases. She touches his hand. Phillip looks in her milky blue eyes, lighted with kindness.

How is the girl? he asks, watching dirty pudgy knees and grass in hair.

A frown crosses Sophia's face. You have not been kind to your mother, have you Annie? she calls to her child. Her throat looked terribly inflamed a few weeks ago. She cried in the night. *Wailed.* She has come good now. I think it is the warmth. I don't know what I would do without her. Sophia twists her neck back to Phillip. You did not tell me who saint Virgil was.

The name is close to me, says Phillip. Virgil is the patron saint of all the Irish who are lost in far-off places. He is the defender of those of us who have come to live at the antipodes.

Sophia does not seem to understand. Did you hear about that prisoner, Alexander Pearce? She tugs a different thread.

Phillip feels like a stone. He had been one of the first to hear. He only whispers: Knopwood informed me after the trial.

I know some prisoners in town, Sophia says, who were transported with him. They tell me it is impossible he is a *cannibal*.

Phillip does not give voice to his thoughts. Of course it is impossible that the prisoner Pearce is a cannibal. No European person could reach such depravity. But then it was supposed to be impossible to escape Macquarie Harbour.

Knopwood told Phillip about the admission a few months ago. In the intervening time, Phillip has adopted the appalling task of defending his catholic parishioners from the slander that they all eat the flesh of their fellows. It is particular to the Irish, whose torturers enjoy making barbs about hunger.

Phillip blames Knopwood's social gluttony for the life of the story, which is now well-known because he could not keep it to himself, even if he did not believe it. Now even children know that Pearce was captured four months after having escaped Macquarie Harbour with seven others, and captured alone. Two of his companions had already returned, after only 12 days, but they perished from exhaustion.

Knopwood did not honour the story, Phillip says by way of explanation to Sophia. The prisoner Pearce was merely covering for his fellow absconders who must still be in the bush. There is no way known that he made it across the interior alone.

He is now back at Macquarie Harbour, Sophia says. Phillip observes a titillating awe in her eye. I wonder if he will escape again.

In the passing weeks, Phillip sits and sighs and masturbates and drinks bad wine. He watches the ships between Hunter Island and the Derwent. He tries to forget about the tall tales that occupy the grotesque gossips of Hobart-town, words of cannibalism and Irish beasts.

In October a public protest is held against the recall of Governor Sorell. Phillip does not graft to protests of any kind, but he signs the appeal that is addressed to His Majesty to request the continuation of the beloved colonel's office. The petition is graciously received, and graciously denied.

Sophia brings Mary Ann up to the church each week, walking from the house of Constable Hellings. Phillip sets his timepiece to her visits.

They will speak about us in town, Phillip says one day by mistake as Sophia arranges Mary Ann's bonnet. Sophia asks how so.

You are here often, Sophia. They must wonder ... Phillip trails. He feels like a fool.

Sophia laughs and finishes the bow beneath three-year-old Mary Ann's chubby chin. I do not think *they* take much notice, she says.

It is good that you visit, says Phillip pouring the tea. A woman should not live alone in Hobart-town.

I do not live alone. She lifts Mary Ann by her arms and sways her from side to side.

Apart from Constable Hellings. I do not like to think of you receiving suitors. Phillip fills two China cups and takes one to his mouth, drawing the steam into his congested nose.

Do you think yourself my saviour? Sophia's words are a surprise. She leaves the tea alone. I do not live alone. Mister Hellings has a brother. John. He is kind to me. He has built his own home. I do not hurry to the random knocking of strange men, Phillip.

Is John convict or free? Phillip asks. Sophia frowns at the hardness his question. Phillip knows the word convict is seldom used in public speech.

What does it matter? I am an imprisoned woman.

Beware of these men, Phillip says, trying to flatten the coarseness in his voice. He fails. I have seen what they do to women in this colony. I care for you.

Yes, it sounds very much like you do, Sophia says in a single breath. What business is it of yours who I choose to live with?

It is God's business.

I am inclined to believe you, Phillip. God has done great things to the men in my life. He killed my first husband, and he took me away from my second. Perhaps he will see fit to do the same to John Hellings, seeing as I am such a prostitute living in his care.

Phillip calls after Sophia but she is already gone. He hurries into the doorway, only to trip over Betty Mack, who stands ignorant and sweet on his doorstep.

Sophia does not look back as she passes the gate.

Betty is courteous enough not to ask. She does not like liquorice tea, but she drinks the abdicate cup. Phillip drags his melancholy eyes from the window which opens onto the outskirts of Hobart-town. After some idle chatter he asks Betty why she has come without her father.

Bobby is resting his eyes, she answers. I could not wait for him to wake. I have news to tell you.

Is she 17 or 18? Phillip cannot recall. He looks into her bright, unsullied eyes. I am to be married to Henry Morrisby of Clarence Plains. She squeaks with excitement. Phillip remembers the boy. He has met him twice.

Bobby must be overjoyed, Phillip offers, attempting excitement. Will he conduct the ceremony?

Of course. And you will attend. I only wish my mother could be there.

She will be watching from afar, Phillip says.

In response Betty raises a bunch of sympathetic white daisies. They are the race of flower from Knopwood's garden. I want to visit her, but I do not want to go alone, she says.

Phillip swirls the leaves in his cup like a school of fish and drains his tea. He collects his coat and top hat from the rack nearby. He donates his hand.

The old burial ground is a green hill skirted by Hobart's low sandy shoal. Knopwood has told Phillip that this was the site of the first church in Hobart-town, a poorly-built timber temple that the colonists had built over the grave of their first governor, the *saint* David Collins. The wind blew that church over. Now the cemetery looks more like a den of thieves than a place of sacred remembrance. There is only one nice spot about it, at the highest part above the broken headstones where a person can see, in one sweep of their neck, the deep southern ocean to the tip of Table Mountain.

Abandoning beauty, Phillip knows that bodies have been discovered there, and not those interred in graves. Phillip walks carefully with Betty between timbers and blocks of stone, like the teeth of a rotten jaw. Betty leads Phillip to a straight board of blue-gum. Phillip presents the pail Betty asked him to bring. Together they fill it with water from the beach and carry it back to the totem, plunging rags in the saltwater and scrubbing away the lichen that has made the words indiscernible. Phillip stands back when the board has been cleaned: *IN MEMORY OF MARY MACK WHO DEPARTED THIS LIFE October 16th 1808 aged 27 YEARS.*

Phillip has heard Knopwood scandalised for adopting Betty Mack, but they have not taken the story from Knopwood. They do not know of Mary Mack, a free woman, however poor, who sailed with governor Collins. They do not know that she took child with one of Collins's marines, and that after he served her so short a duty, that he was discharged to England, never to return. They do not know that Betty was eight month old when Knopwood took her and her mother in. Mary died a few months later.

Phillip cares not for the criticism of another man of God. He would be a hypocrite to deaden the flower of Knopwood's achievements on no other ground but infertility. After all, what children does Phillip have to boast of? What wife? He is thankful that he is surrounded by syphilis and sin else it might be more difficult than it is. He tells himself he does it for God.

It is for God he took the charge, disguised as an honour in the beginning, to sail from the old world to the new, which somehow feels darker and more eld than any district he ever knew in the barren fields of Ireland.

He looks across the cemetery and catches eyes with a small gathering of woollen-backed rogues. Their faces are unshaven and their looks distracted. Phillip thinks of Sophia. If only he could tell her he does not wish to carve her name into a slab of blue-gum for the crimes of a vagrant man.

Phillip looks again across the cemetery. The gathering of three men stand in the shadows of a large stone mausoleum. Then a fourth hunched body appears, crouching, his hands on his britches. Phillip feels suddenly sick.

Betty, come with me, he says, reaching for her hand. He raises his walking cane. He shouts at the men but they are gone, darting into the bush along the waterline. Phillip hurries to the stone block, dragging Betty behind him. He finds a woman in the grass.

Her woollen dress is torn, exposing her breasts, and a felt hat is pressed onto her face. Phillip kneels in the grass and removes the hat with caution.

Christ, Johanna.

He takes her bruised face in his hands. She mumbles something, her eyes three quarters shut. Phillip sits her gently against the stone block and passes his greatcoat about her shoulders, buttoning it up at the front. He keeps Betty close.

Do not go away from me, he says. Then he places Johanna Lynch's hands on his walking cane and pulls her to her feet. Her black head is loose at the neck. Phillip summons all his will to carry her.

When they come into a street behind the gaol grounds, Phillip sends Betty to find a constable or soldier. She returns with two constables. Together they carry Johanna to the hospital.

It takes her a week to recover. Every day Phillip visits her, taking fresh beans from his garden for her to chew. Colour returns to her face, though her oily black hair cannot be straightened. When the warden discharges her, Phillip informs him that the woman is in his care.

As they walk from the hospital together he leans into Johanna and asks, Where is your man Cavanagh? Johanna doesn't reply. When they come into the street, Phillip faces his feet in the direction of St Virgil's church. Johanna pulls away.

I must go tend to my children, she says.

Phillip asks if they are with their father.

John is never at home, Johanna complains. Brigid is now two and a half. And I have an infant on milk. They must stay with another family while I … work.

Phillip gives her a thorough look. He contemplates her words for a long time. Do not tell me there is no other path but to make a prostitute of yourself.

Johanna does not flinch.

I do not care about myself, it is my children I fear for. It is them that need feeding.

Come and stay with me, Phillip perseveres. I can put you and your children up at St Virgil's for as long as you need.

Johanna's eyes moisten. I cannot, she says, blinking. I cannot take the children from John.

He is never home. He is not with you. He did not *protect* you. He has given up his right to be a father.

What right is parenthood? Johanna mourns. It is a sentence. She pauses while some people pass them with looks. Phillip draws closer to her, although his hands remain at his sides. Johanna's sad eyes bring him pain, more than the crack on her lip or the shrinking bump on her forehead. She goes on, enchanted a little: The world renews itself, Phillip. Every year the magpies are born. A farmer will sew and harvest. New children cry. Why do the pains of us not disappear like old and ageing parents?

It is as you say, Phillip replies, thinking as he speaks, the world renews itself. The pains of us are crops—they may disappear when reaped by one, but are destined to return for another. We sow our own troubles. Phillip reaches into his jacket and produces his bible. He holds it as an example. That is why God's Word endures. Our pains have been the same since the days of Adam.

Johanna's face is a twist. She screws up her mouth and spits on the black cover of Phillip's bible.

Phillip withdraws as though a viper has lunged at him. His sympathy withers. He gathers the bible between two fingers, saliva dripping. He scowls at the woman, unable to speak. She strips off his greatcoat and drops it in the street, leaving the priest and his bible alone.

CUTHBERTSON

Macquarie Harbour, 1823 A.D.

Cuthbertson wakes from one of the finest sleeps of his life. He is only a little dry in the mouth, so he collects a skin from his writing desk. A comb of afternoon sunlight drips between ruffled curtains. He does not feel like himself – heady uninterrupted sleep has always been so foreign in his years. He tastes something of promotion in the rare afternoon nap.

He takes a long key and unlocks the lowest drawer in his desk. He moves aside the pistol wrapped in cloth and takes out a broken letter. He carries it to the southeast window to read again.

The curtain retreats with his hand. Down on the docks the logging gangs are returning. They look doleful. Cuthbertson admits to himself that he cannot fathom where they find the stones to contemplate escape after such days. It would not help if he could understand. They are like frightened sheep. No, they are, perhaps, less like sheep and more like tygers, infernal, ugly poachers, worth next to nothing; though the bounty for a tyger is five shillings – seven if female. This is more than the worth of any convict.

Cuthbertson has discovered a joke. He writes the words convict and tyger on a scrap of paper so he remembers it. They are both striped, in their own ways, both thieving, both strung up to display their lack of place in the civilised world.

Cuthbertson was young but he can still remember when the last wolf was killed in Ireland. A cousin or an uncle took him to see it. It lay dead on the frosted grass. It already looked as though its mottled fur had been filled with stuffing. The Year of Our Lord 1796, he thinks. A celebrated year. The last beast gone, the world at last tamed.

But that did not let the sheep grow. That did not feed the masses.

Cuthbertson screws up the paper and tosses it in the cold snow of the hearth. He wonders what they will say about the last tyger, if it will even be remembered, if its absence will make the colony any healthier, or relieve any afflictions now in place. At least the tyger and the wolf can be hunted to extinction; the criminal is born, bred of the mind, unpredictably spawned, and clothed in the same skin as righteous men.

The lash can prune sentiment, but Cuthbertson is at a loss as to how the government can stay the birth of criminals. Alas, he thinks, poring over his letter, that question is no longer his burden. His time is drawing to a close. Cuthbertson fingers the broken seal, the three arms of the government broad arrow. He has read the letter so many times since it arrived that he can almost recite it from mind. A man named Wright, a lieutenant much like himself, is scheduled to replace him in the summer of the following year. Cuthbertson will be the gate keeper of hell no longer.

He is roused from his thoughts by a knock on the door.

Cuthbertson dresses quickly. It is Sergeant Waddy.

Lieutenant, sir. Smoke has been sighted near Pine Cove Point.

Cuthbertson retrieves his spyglass and steps outside. From the foreshore he sees a frail fume rising behind the brows of a distant coastline, in the nor'west along King's River. Cuthbertson's first instinct is escape, but he drags his spyglass along the horizon and can see no signal fires. He remembers the escape more than a year ago when eight including that runt Alexander Pearce had fled over the mountains. Two returned with the pots and axes they escaped with, but they were too spent to speak. It should have brought Cuthbertson joy when he heard the news of Pearce's eventual capture – except that it meant his return to Macquarie Harbour.

Knopwood should have known the danger of sending a famous absconder back to his former prison. Cuthbertson is antagonised by the memory of Pearce's haughty face. He prioritised the punishment of his fame so that others did not think there was any reward in escape. He was always on the triangle and frequently alone upon the small island. But for all his weakness, Cuthbertson confesses in a very deep and hidden part of him that, like Huon pine, Pearce is soaked in something so stubborn it denies all efforts to break it apart.

Just nine days prior has the wretch absconded again, with another prisoner – Cuthbertson thinks his name Cox. That is the real joke, that prisoners, in full knowledge fire will burn them, like children, think the second time it might be cool.

This time Cuthbertson hopes Pearce is dead. If Pearce ever returns again, he will make sure of it.

The smoke is too far up the coast to be a signal fire, says Cuthbertson. Without an alternative suggestion he gathers Waddy together with some privates and they set off to investigate the smoke.

The afternoon already thins like enamel on a black pot. The wind comes on very cold. It is a far way to go in just the whaler they are in, but Cuthbertson's schooner is not ready yet. She requires final touches before he will set her free. At any rate, he is not worried. It is yet late November – December is known for the worst storms.

Dusk is upon them, but before the day vanishes, taking the pillar of smoke with it, Cuthbertson sights a government ship.

'Tis the *Waterloo*, says Sergeant Waddy.

The pilot Lucas must see them in the twilit water for a naval bell peals on-board the vessel. Cuthbertson's whaler draws aside. He clutches a ladder which is cast down from the deck.

Lieutenant, Lucas does not veil his surprise.

Have you found the source of the smoke? Cuthbertson does not waste the waning day.

The main deck of the *Waterloo* is all in lanterns. Gold touches only Lucas's pronounced features. The rest of his face is grey.

Alexander Pearce, the pilot says gravely. We discovered him on the shore of Pine Cove Point. He had lit a fire and smothered it so the signal would catch our attention. I sailed five miles aside to investigate, and sent a boat to the shore.

Lucas does not whisper, but his voice is at half measure and Cuthbertson wonders why.

I recognised Pearce when I came ashore. Christ, he was queer. His jacket was his own, with the number 102 on it, but his shirt and everything else was another prisoner's. I asked him, Pearce, why have you another man's number on? Then I remembered he had escaped with Cox.

Pearce said very quickly that Cox was drowned in King's River. I said if Cox was drowned why was his jacket wet and Cox's undergarments which he wore dry. Then I had him searched.

Lucas whispers now. There was not much on him but spoiled half-eaten food. There was a strange fillet in his jacket – like something dead of the deep sea. He seemed at a loss when I pulled it out, like he had forgotten about it.

He said, again very quick, that it was a piece of Cox, and Cox had been drowned. He said it was to prove he had died. I did not say another word to him after that.

Good God, says Cuthbertson. Where is he?

Lucas steps aside and gestures to a putrid creature lying on the deck. The top of his coiled mass is yellow with lantern and the rest is darkling. Three men with guns stand at hand. Pearce lifts his ragged head and sits up as Cuthbertson approaches. He looks either indifferent or confused, Cuthbertson cannot tell.

Cuthbertson addresses him in a rising voice, standing straight and tall. The convict's wandering eyes are now petrified.

Pearce, you will tell me now why you were carrying Cox's flesh in your pockets. Why are you dressed in his clothes?

Pearce does not have a voice at first. He repeats: Cox was drowned in the river. I cut a piece of flesh as a proof he is dead. He does not need his clothes any more. He is drowned.

Cuthbertson has no patience. The humour of his fine sleep is evaporated. He thinks of privates Reynolds and Parker, long gone. He looks upon Cox's number on Pearce's garments. He thinks of the story that came back with Pearce's return, denied by Robert Knopwood as incomprehensible.

Alexander Pearce, did you do the deed? Cuthbertson asks with low gravel. Now he yells: Did you do it!

Pearce is straightened by his thunder. He quivers. He says yes.

They spend the evening aboard the *Waterloo* with the whaleboat roped to the hull. It knocks, wood on wood. It is the only sound in the night. Pearce lays roped to the mast. As dawn bleeds on the water, Cuthbertson orders his coxswain Smith to take Pearce ashore and recover Cox's body.

He hears the pulsing tide as he waits. He is desperate for evidence that will send Pearce away forever. He cannot have this on his conscience when he retires from Macquarie Harbour.

He sees Smith on the sand, stepping now into the whaleboat. Smith holds a tool in his hands – an axe. Pearce comes behind him. There is a grimy filthy rug in his arms.

When Cuthbertson has seen enough he returns to Settlement Island. There is not enough of Cox for a Christian burial, but it doesn't matter. There is dead flesh at least, and Smith has found an axe; both of those things will seal Cuthbertson's recommendation that Pearce be hanged.

Upon arrival at Settlement Island, Smith asks if they should hide the remains. Cuthbertson's order is clear: Make it known to all.

With Cox's remains he will sear away Pearce's heroics and the suggestion that escape is at all possible. Cuthbertson makes a couple of prisoners known to Pearce, Lawton and Letting, carry the reeking bundles in disgust. Every eye bears witness. They all see mangled, jaundiced Pearce walk behind his old mates, retching as they hobble. They all know he escaped with Cox. They had saluted him for it.

Now you see.

Cuthbertson hurries. He must write a letter to the governor. The arrival of prisoners has been appalling and haphazard to date, but Cuthbertson knows that when the next ship comes, he will be sending one back. He drafts the letter and calls his clerk Douglas. He will speak with Pearce a final time so that, no matter how many lies he spins in the future, he will not be able to escape his past.

★ ★ ★

Pearce's face is empty when Cuthbertson arrives in the hospital. It is not the face of a killer. It is the face of a nervous child.

Douglas, take up a pen, Cuthbertson orders his scribe.

Cuthbertson tells Pearce he knows what became of Kennerly and Brown — he says they died on these very tables in this hospital room — but he asks what happened to the others, the first time.

Pearce, without a bush to hide in, gives Cuthbertson what he asks for. When he comes to the death of Dalton, Cuthbertson feels bidden to whisper Jesus's name for protection.

There is no minor plot here, thinks Cuthbertson, as Pearce drags his tale forward. There is barely enough for a story. Bodenham and Mather were killed the same way: murder and digestion. For a change of pace, Travers was bitten on the foot by a snake, after which Greenhill carried him for days until he died, black and blue. Then there was only Pearce and Greenhill. Cuthbertson is told by Pearce that he murdered Greenhill only in his sleep, but Cuthbertson has arrived at a place where he cannot sift truth from lies.

After Greenhill, Pearce describes to Cuthbertson the fatty taste of raw duck. The wild game and small sheep of the reedy marshes west of the Ouse River – his salvation. He says that he was taken in by a bushranger he had met before, although the man nearly shot him for a stranger – this is how gaunt his skin was, how parched his eyes, his dirty beard like a skeleton's. He says he soaked his bones in the warmth of the flames of the hut, feeling like a husk of a living thing, or a snake curled up in the winter sun.

When he regained himself he found old companions, Davis and Churton, and they ranged together as they had done before. But the freebooting did not last, and when he was arraigned before the court, Pearce admits that he thought everyone already knew the things that he had done. He did not know Kennerly and Brown had not lived to speak. Dead men tell no tales.

Cuthbertson smokes his pipe into the small hours of the morning. While his candle lasts, he holds a stick of sealing wax over the flame until it drips fat tears onto an envelope. He folds Douglas's account, places it inside, and presses down the government broad arrow. He puts this aside.

He takes up the correspondence that he knows by heart. His relief. Lieutenant Wright to replace him. But there is one concern: the missive holds no words about promotion. Surely he will not return to the road-gang? Perhaps his elevation is yet to come. He is due to leave at Christmas. No matter his fate, his lasting gift to Macquarie Harbour is the conquest of its cannibals. Surely no convict will escape after them.

Presently, as Cuthbertson's oil lamp is flawed by his thick draught, he suffers the memory of Pearce's parting words.

Are you ready to die, Pearce? Cuthbertson had asked as he made to leave the hospital.

The shadows in the orb of the lamp upon the ceiling are like

Pearce's eyes. They moved onto him with weight which remains. He spoke in Irish: I died when I came here. Cuthbertson did not speak back to him, but he could not help his mind as it recognised the words, heirlooms of a language that he cannot forget.

CONOLLY

Hobart-town, 1824 A.D.

Phillip did not see Johanna Lynch for the remainder of 1823. St Virgil's was consecrated, and regular mass taken, but Phillip felt empty.

He has now trespassed on many months of the new year and still he feels empty. Betty Mack comes to Phillip's church regularly, a habit which started after the incident in the cemetery last year. Phillip is not much comfort to her. He is hardly comfort to himself. He masturbates every day. Sunday is not the day of rest in this case. He does not have much to draw on, so he seizes spry moments of unexplained arousal.

Reverend! He jolts at the call of Betty Mack's voice. He screws up the rag in his hand and tosses it behind a pew. He pulls his cassock down over his spread legs.

Just scrubbing my rosary beads, he says touching his forehead with a handkerchief – Phillip checks twice to make sure it is clean.

I can come back. Betty appears in the doorway with a benign smile on her face. There is a basket in her arms.

Phillip stands awkwardly. No, your timing is splendid Betty. I just finished my last hail Mary.

Sometimes Phillip wishes she wouldn't come around so often. He would not feel defiled if Betty hadn't walked in. He snatches a nearby slate and nub of chalk from his pocket and notes to discuss with God if sexual guilt has something to do with the judgement of others. Now he is thinking unnecessarily of Robert Knopwood and he has returned to the usually torpid state his holy robes prefer.

Mister and Mis'ess Hellings will be by shortly. Betty calls Sophia Mis'ess Hellings although she is not married to John. Phillip wonders if Betty practises this ignorance on purpose or if she is a genuine child. He does not remember that they arranged lunch, but it is not the first time he has forgotten.

Phillip thinks Sophia has forgiven him, although she has not put her amnesty into words. Phillip has not apologised either, but their quiet language of swift touches and subtle expressions says enough. Phillip's flock is not company for him. He could not countenance being a shepherd up in the backblocks. He needs Sophia.

Over the months Phillip has suffered the presence of John Hellings, though he looks like a man Phillip would avoid in the street. He wonders if Sophia has taken up with him to mend the loss of her daughter's father. It should not be a thought in his mind. Phillip is not her brother. He is not even her parson. He cannot control her actions. Her choices are her own.

The venue for lunch would normally be Knopwood's Cottage Green, but he has been ill so they meet without him. It is only Sophia and her Mary Ann, Betty Mack and John Hellings. Hellings treads on Phillip's good hospitality by regurgitating the only conversation Phillip does not wish to hear.

Alexander Pearce arrived today, Hellings announces as Sophia stuffs a gamebird. She stops with her hand lost in the pallid flesh. Phillip trades glances with her.

Hellings is not sensitive to their trade. He pares away the foil on a bottle of brandy with his fingernail as though it is the most accomplished skill he has – he is butchering it.

You'd better open that bottle quicker than I can say Jack Robertson, Phillip says in a low voice.

My brother told me so, Hellings advises, finally parting the bottle from its top.

Robinson, Sophia says to Phillip. Quicker than Jack Robinson is the saying. You said Robertson.

Phillip fills four tumblers. I must have been thinking of someone, Phillip says in a ponder. He remembers what the convicts call Lieutenant Cuthbertson of the 48th regiment but does not voice it. He fills four tumblers and drinks two quicker than anyone can say Robinson or Robertson.

The *Duke of York* berthed a day or two ago, Hellings elaborates. The constables what escorted Pearce to gaol says he murdered somebody at Macquarie Harbour. They say he *ate* the man he killed.

'Tis a story, Phillip replies. Why must the bodies of this colony be so obsessed with ungodly yarns? They talk so much about this rubbish ... I can see they will write books about it. I wish they wouldn't. Did you know he's from Monaghan?

Hellings shakes his head. Sophia's eyes examine Phillip. He notices the touch of her eyes which question if he knows more about Alexander Pearce than he lets on.

Every person in the colony knows what he confessed to Knopwood about his first escape, says Hellings. Now he has done it again. He will pay for it this time. My brother—

Phillip lifts a forbidding hand. Charming, John, truly. But for the sake of the poor bird with Miss Nightingale's hand in its behind, can we shelve these terrible tales? Sophia laughs and Betty Mack removes her hands from Mary Ann's juvenile ears.

Hellings grins too, but it is confected. He may not like Phillip referring to Sophia by her maiden name. Sophia scrubs her greasy herbed fingers with a cloth. Phillip is gripped by the memory of the dirty rag behind the pew. There is no slate for him to write a reminder to clean it up before it walks out his church on the sole of a parishioner.

In March, the month before Sorell is due to depart, Phillip finds himself in a room of government house sharing drinks. They are awaiting the arrival of the new chief justice.

Be ready, my friend, Sorell's spirited breath boasts without discretion. For seven years I have campaigned for this colony to become its own. In July, the house of commons at home passed the law that will make it so.

Phillip thinks it strange to hear Sorell refer to Britain as *at home,* although he does not wonder where Sorell will return to once his duty is ended.

We will have our supreme court by the middle of this year. Even if I am not here to see it. We will have the authority to stamp our own law.

And hang our own criminals, Phillip thinks.

Phillip regards Sorell, tipping himself dangerously close to the tides of the punchbowl. He feels in a sudden as though he is the soberest person at the soiree. He is alarmed that Sorell believes the new court to be his *legacy.*

Each man feels that history has existed solely that it may produce him, at his moment, in his place, Phillip says with a carefully painted tincture of respect. He speaks slowly, wary of anger and hopeful that the governor admires him enough to credit his advice. I firmly believe that this line of thinking is what separates us from animals. It is a selfish thought and a terrific danger. Sorell's round hospitable eyes have not changed. For a cruel man, it means he feels justified as the tyrant of his own hell—even the well-intentioned man might find himself a tyrant by no fault of his own. Take the statesmen of England who devised this experiment, intent on saving the wretched half of our generation. I think even you can agree, sir, that we would be making the best the enemy of the good to pretend that they have done a fine job.

Sorell smiles and nods and his eyes do not change.

Phillip is thinking of Lieutenant John Cuthbertson and all the stories he has heard, but he does not mention that name. He knows Sorell appointed him.

These people will be awfully disappointed when they learn—if they learn—that history has not chosen them specially. If it wasn't their foot in the boot, it would be someone else's foot, if you catch my drift.

He expects anger or thoughtful discussion, but not indifference. Sorell slaps him on the shoulder and says haughtily, Leave decisions of the state to statesmen, reverend.

He has always liked that he can speak to Sorell like a member of the commons, but being a man for all seasons has its shortcomings if it trespasses on conviction. Phillip is certain the governor is the one who misunderstands.

On the 10th of April the annual Agricultural Show is held at the market place. It is one month to the day before the supreme court is to open. Sorell is not long to the colony now. Accordingly, *Colonel Sorell* is the toast of the occasion, and when 50 wealthy gentlemen raise their glasses to the pavilion and proclaim the health of the governor, Phillip thinks their cheers will never cease. However, it is as though some spirit arrives, intent on breaking apart Phillip's solace, when one of the gentlemen present mentions the name of Alexander Pearce. Phillip's cock-tail loses all its flavour.

Phillip first heard that Pearce was a Monaghan native from Bobby Knopwood, born six miles from where he had been born. Phillip fights the creeping notion that there is any common blood between them. *Six miles*, he ponders as protestant landowners gossip around him. Phillip thinks back to his childhood. How far away Van Diemen's Land was then, only an island from books of fantasy. Phillip could not have known he was born six miles from the crib of a cannibal. Phillip now thinks it an uncanny twist of fate that Pearce will die six feet from where he stands.

The name of John Cuthbertson is folded into his personal mind, independent of the festivities – perhaps a flying word or mention from some nearby conversation has prompted him to think of Pearce's gaoler. He illustrates a strange mental image of a long beam with Pearce at one end and Cuthbertson on the other. In the middle the beam lies across Phillip's own arms. An axis of brothers, not quite good and evil. He wonders how different life would be if John Cuthbertson was a catholic priest and Phillip himself a protestant soldier. He crosses himself twice. The very thought is a heresy. It is a heresy to question what would have to change for it to be him in the Hobart-town gaol and Alexander Pearce in holy robes at the governor's going away party with a timber doodle in his hand.

Phillip sips his cock-tail and thinks it a stupid name for a drink. He would laugh about the irony of holding a timber doodle in his hand if he didn't think half the women in Hobart-town *actually* thought he had a one. Now he questions the mirth of the barman who looked him up and down and chuckled when Phillip said: I cannot turn down a timber doodle. He thought the barman was drunk, now he thinks of his unclean rosary beads and Betty Mack, and he would much rather be anywhere else than the Agricultural Show.

In the whimsy of these thoughts he is sobered by an alarming realisation when he sees the new chief justice across the room. The seesaw reappears in his mind. He understands why Pearce, brought back to Hobart-town some time ago, has been left to languish in gaol all the months since. He was not sent to Sydney to face trial as a murderer. The government would save the expense. He is to be the first man executed by the colony's supreme court.

Pearce is not the last dead man to be brought back from Macquarie Harbour. Nine days after the festivities of the Agricultural Show, a schooner lays anchor in the bay. Phillip hears that it brings the body of a soldier back from the west. Phillip cannot attend the funeral, the procession of which he can see from his doorstep. On a discomforting wind he catches the faint dirge of a military band. It is not the music he wishes to hear.

Mary Ann Nightingale has taken ill. The surgeon, James Scott, who returned for the funeral, visits on Phillip's special request, but his only recommendation is surgery. Scott warns the procedure will likely take the life of the child, due to her age.

Phillip cannot bear Sophia's smarting face as Scott speaks. He explains the requisite surgery, and she cries because she does not understand. Her eyes are scarred by tear-tracked cheeks when Scott leaves. Mary Ann's red face is like a folded rose in her arms. Phillip, she whispers. Can you pray for her as you prayed on the *Janus*?

Phillip sings to the child, but he feels powerless. He calls on God, but hears no answer.

In three and a half weeks the new chief justice is raised to the bench of the supreme court. But Phillip is not in town to witness it. He makes a hermitage of St Virgil's, and only visits Sophia at the house of John Hellings.

On the 13th day of May, Betty Mack comes to Phillip's cottage to tell him about the new governor's arrival. Phillip is actually praying this time. She dispenses with all the colourful details of Governor Arthur's landing: a salute of 13 guns and the thunderheads of 32-pound cannon from the battery; the officers in Turkey red and their wives in plunging London dresses. Phillip cares to ask one question: Is his wife *his wife* or another man's? Betty does not know the answer.

For want of a response she says she knows by way of Bobby, who heard it from some prisoners, that Colonel Arthur is a flagitious fiend. Betty says she does not think he looks so evil, not dressed in gold and crimson. Phillip looks at her with pity.

Mary Ann dies on the 23rd day of May. It is a Sunday. Phillip has just finished his mass when John Hellings hurries into the church. Phillip's lungs burn with cold air as he runs ahead.

There is no mention of her death in the papers that Betty Mack brings to Phillip's draughty cottage. Betty does not linger. Phillip takes his tea alone now. He attends Mary Ann's funeral every morning when he wakes and every evening when he lowers his head. Knopwood is with him in those dreams. Sophia kneels in the dewy grass. John Hellings and his brother lower a quarter-sized coffin into the ground. The memory cannot be rebuked.

Phillip has not felt this amount of pain before, at least in many long years, not in such a specific part of his body that is not his heart and not his stomach — it is somewhere untouchable.

Phillip can say nothing to comfort Sophia when he sees her. He cannot even comfort himself. She asks him why God injures children. He says it is not God's doing. He says mankind has brought sin into the world, and that mankind must live with sin until Jesus Christ returns. Sophia asks him when that will be.

In the absence of comforting words, he sings in Irish, and does not care who hears him; in Irish he can ask God why, and the others will not hear his doubts.

The farewell banquet for Governor Sorell is held a fortnight after Mary Ann's death. Phillip does not attend, but he is present on the shore when his friend and benefactor sets sail. Sorell stands in the whaleboat and waves emphatically with both arms, as the winding oars pull him towards the masts of a barque. He becomes smaller in the grey-green waves. Phillip asks himself how well he actually knows the tiny man in the little yellow boat. He thinks of Sorell's round indifferent eyes. He wonders how indifferent the new governor will be. He would rather not meet George Arthur, but he knows he has no choice. He knows the day will arrive soon.

CONOLLY

Hobart-town, June 1824 A.D.

It may be the second Friday in June but Phillip cannot remember. It has been weeks since he has shaved and people are beginning to talk. He inspects the speckled wings of his nose. He scrapes them with a fingernail. The skin beneath his eyes is purple. Even to him, his cowled eyes seem resigned. He is in no state to meet the governor. He looks across to the nightstand where the letter lies.

Phillip does not care to make an impression on the man – a depressed malady has stricken him lately – but he is aware that a harmonious relationship with the governor is crucial to his ministry. Although he puts faith in Sorell's recommendation, only in person will George Arthur approve his character.

He rides on horseback through town towards government house, having dressed in black trowsers, a waistcoat and his cleanest overcoat. A pewter crucifix jumps on a tether around his neck. He crosses town alone, accompanied only by vague indifferent souls. The sea is swollen and grey, far away to Phillip's right, beyond the swaying masts of the tall ships. He encourages his dull horse down the hill with the impotent flip of a riding crop. The naval bells in the grey green bight below haunt the air.

Phillip meets the new governor in the sitting room of government house. They are the same age or within a few years of one another. Phillip is now 38. He feels every one in his bones. As for Arthur, the years have drawn back his hairline. A high white forehead gleams. Sober grey eyes brood beneath charcoal brows. He does not smile. There is a curl at the edges of his mouth but it is not a smile.

Arthur wears a night-blue satin neckerchief and a navy frockcoat undone. Beneath is a white, double-breasted shirt with gold buttons. His trowsers are linen, his legs crossed. Phillip thinks they look like chess pieces, a bishop and a king facing one another across the board.

Arthur sits opposite Phillip with a missive in his hand. It is unheard of, he proclaims three times, looking at Phillip square.

They speak of one matter alone.

Will you take a drink, Conolly? Arthur asks, raising a glass in his right hand. Phillip salivates but abstains. He only debauches in the privacy of friends. He does not think he will be friends with this governor.

I assume you know why I have summoned you, Arthur goes on.

You know I will be confessor to the condemned, sir.

Arthur sets his glass aside. Half true. I know you are Irish, and he is Irish.

Governor, I had no idea I had been found out. Phillip cannot help himself.

Arthur's face does not change. Being an Irishman, surely you understand my concern.

I'm afraid I don't, your excellency; that I and this Alexander Pearce were born to the same Ireland means nothing – I have never met the man.

O, but I would wager there are plenty in this colony who know your name without ever having met you, reverend. You are a whimpering candle for them. You may not provide warmth where they lay at night, but they see your light all the same, and for the catholics, that faint light is just enough. They may say: Conolly, he is our man in this southern land. One thing Sorell told me before he retired his station: Conolly will be your greatest asset in bringing the settlement to heel, and not only for the catholics. He is an excellent adjudicator, and a tireless preacher, even if he is Irish.

Phillip does not take tireless as a compliment. He *feels* tired.

Sorell was generous with his praise, Phillip says dismissively through a grimace. Were he less generous to the wives of other men, perhaps you and I would not be having this conversation.

Sorell made no exaggeration, Conolly. The entire settlement is the better for having you here.

Phillip is sensitive to the sudden deception of flattery. What do you require of me, governor, here and now? You did ask for my person.

To the point. Forthrightness. An admirable quality. No, you're absolutely right. Arthur's leather chair creaks as he reclines. I wanted to make sure we are cut of the same cloth, so to speak … about this Pearce. I know he is a countryman of yours. I want to be sure he's going to take the gallows in silence.

I can assure you, Phillip begins with spice, that I share no common trait with a cannibal, whether he is Irish-born or not. You needn't worry about fraternity in the gaol cell or rowdy Irish brothers on the hanging platform. I've no doubts the devil lives in the words of such a sinner, and I will not make myself party to that.

Rain begins to patter on the window. Phillip wonders if he has been too brash when the door in the hallway whines. The parlour is filled with two more guests, an ailing man led by the arm of a young woman. Phillip cannot secret his smile.

Reverend Knopwood, you're early, Arthur says with the slightest frustration.

Is that an Irish voice I hear? Knopwood remarks with a smack of his loosening lips.

It is true what they say about the powerful other-senses of the blind, Phillip says in reply.

Arthur snaps a curious look, the draught of which Phillip can feel. The governor's concern abates when Knopwood laughs and reaches sightlessly for Phillip's hand.

We were discussing the matter of Alexander Pearce, Arthur reiterates slowly, watching Knopwood and Phillip's handshake with interest.

Phillip leans towards Betty and wishes good afternoon in her ear.

He is to go before the new supreme court one week to the day, tried for the capital offence of murder. *Murder* only. I hear a man cannot be tried for cannibalism if his witnesses have all been eaten, Knopwood says.

Hearing is not a substitute for seeing, Robert, says Phillip, a little frustrated.

You know he confessed to me last time, Knopwood charges ahead. Betty helps him down onto the sofa. Though his eyes are failing, Phillip can see in his twitching countenance the kind of gross fascination he is sure will permeate Pearce's narrative. Knopwood is a proper gentleman but not immune to the scent of the macabre. It is a fume that tantalises the nostrils of all people, no matter their class.

You could not have heard his confession, Robert. You are not a catholic. Phillip is more aggravated now.

I heard his case, nonetheless – Knopwood wobbles a hand in the air – when I was at the bar. But it was nothing more than a fiction to me then.

So you returned him to Sarah Island, Arthur reunites with the conversation.

You would have done the same, colonel, Knopwood says plaintively, shifting in his seat. Honesty is so rare in the breed of bondsmen that even his apparent admission seemed to be a lie. I did not know what we know now, how they ended up, those seven fellows he escaped with.

For all Colonel Sorell's great endeavours, gentlemen, announces Arthur, I do question the usefulness of Macquarie Harbour.

He led them to the body, you know, alights Knopwood on his own tangent.

Must we? Betty's high voice falls between them. I came for afternoon tea. If I wanted a spectacular tale I would have stayed indoors with a book.

I agree with Miss Mack, Phillip concurs with relief, eager to find the shortest passage away from Alexander Pearce.

You are made of sterner stuff than that, surely Phillip, Knopwood says without sensitivity.

I have not the stomach for it today. I've walked many a man to the gallows, reverend, as have you. It is not something we relish, but it is a charge that we execute for the pleasure of God, and the sake of our king. But I will not tempt the devil with talk like this.

Phillip can see from the corner of his eye he has curried the governor's approval with these words. Nonetheless, he feels the outsider. He has no interest in chewing the fat with a blind reverend and a visionary governor. But we keep the company that feeds us, he thinks, and Arthur is now his paymaster.

When only crumbs are left on the plates, Betty expresses her desire to leave, while the rain is at a distance. She excuses with courtesy.

Let me walk you both out, Phillip offers. He opens the door before receiving a stiff look from the governor.

I will be in the refuge, informs Arthur. He turns away and dashes Phillip's bid to leave.

Phillip steps outside with Knopwood and Betty and holds up the reverend's wayward hand, in search of a parting shake.

When we see each other again you will have met with a cannibal. Knopwood's notation is again too trivial to please Phillip. I await your observations. Betty lays a kiss on Phillip's cheek and the pair depart.

Arthur's refuge smells of malt and smoke, leather and the musk of fur. The head of a stag watches over the open fire. Beneath its gilt rack of antlers a red chesterfield glares into the nook, accompanied by a settee wherefrom the governor takes a decanter in his hand. He pours Phillip a glass without asking.

Arthur's deep black boots grin with the fire's gold and the buckles of his uniform shine like medallions. His eyes are pregnant with desire.

Pearce's execution has not yet been scheduled. He stands before the court in a week. I have given explicit instruction that the matter of execution be fully stamped and sealed before the date is scheduled. I do not want there to be any disagreement from Sydney on my authority to exact justice here.

Phillip looks at the governor and sees the epilogue of Sorell's upsets. Arthur will not be chastised by the governor in chief, ever reminded that he is *lieutenant*-governor only. He will be fully enfranchised by the law, and he will show that Van Diemen's Land is no longer the midden heap of New South Wales.

You will hear when the date is scheduled. We likely have a month. Be prepared. Prepare Pearce. And confess for him. Whether he is penitent or not. Do not let him speak for himself. I want his confession to be lasting. Impressive. I want all the convicts who watch that taut strand of rope to know that their crimes will be judged twice over: here in life, and after their death.

Phillip fills his mouth with burning whiskey so that he may have an excuse for silence. Arthur seems satisfied. He has disclosed what he set out to say. Phillip is to be a mouthpiece for the government. He must show that Pearce will be damned whilst making an earnest effort to save him. He is not sure this can be done, because even he is unsure a man like Pearce can be saved – it is easier to see him damned. It is all up to God, but Phillip has felt separate from God lately.

Phillip drains his glass and in quick succession withdraws his pocket watch. This time Arthur lets him leave.

Visit again, the governor farewells, alluding that he will ask again. Phillip communicates his thankyous and then the residence is closed. Betty had left at the opportune time. Phillip now peers across the foreshore and sees a storm galloping towards him from the west. It will catch him before he reaches his door. The tiers behind the pipe organ rocks of Table Mountain are black and angry. Phillip pulls his collar and makes haste with the reins.

CUTHBERTSON

Macquarie Harbour, December 1823 A.D.

Do you know what night this is? Lieutenant Cuthbertson asks as he pours his first draught of Bengal rum.

Christmas Eve, sir, Douglas answers, hoping for a drink he will not get.

It is my seven hundred and twenty-seventh night on this godforsaken island. Cuthbertson fills five other glasses in anticipation. I've counted every one. His voice shrinks to a solemn whisper.

Douglas is quiet. When Cuthbertson looks up from stopping the ewer, he feels quizzed. Douglas, what is it?

You're smiling, sir.

Cuthbertson gives an emphatic laugh. He reaches inside his coat and pulls out a letter with a broken broad arrow seal. He drops it on the table. Douglas leans in gingerly and reviews the twisted wax. Is it a Christmas letter from the governor?

Cuthbertson cannot tell if the clerk is making a joke. He

hears voices on the path to his door. That is my relief, he corrects, gesturing to the letter. Lieutenant Wright of the 3rd regiment is coming to take my place.

Are you leaving the colony?

I am not being expelled. I am being honoured, Douglas. Jesus. For a moment Cuthbertson feels a disquieting pang of doubt. Decoration could be expected after such a post, and a service so taxing, but the letter made no mention of promotion. There is a rap on the door.

Spry James Kelly and the pilot Lucas enter together. In a few moments the surgeon arrives followed by Jane Waddy with her sergeant husband at hand.

You're rosy, lieutenant sir, Kelly remarks reaching for his predestined rum. Waddy confirms. Cuthbertson directs them both to the letter which Kelly pinches away, running under his swift eye before passing over to Mis'ess Waddy. You're leaving us, sir, says Kelly.

Cuthbertson knows his grin is foreign to them. He shows them to their seats in the cramped parlour that adjoins the main room. He finishes his rum and folds his tongue back over itself to prolong the flavour. It is a rationing habit. He thought he may have a couple of glasses for the occasion, but no more on account of his sober policy. Now he asks, what will sobriety matter after I am gone? He pours another.

Is it the captaincy for you then? Waddy asks from an armchair. Captain Cuthbertson.

Kelly says it sounds dignified.

It sounds well overdue, Cuthbertson clarifies. I was telling Douglas as you arrived, this is my seven hundred and twenty-seventh night upon this island. Cuthbertson is not sure if he sees Kelly wink at the sergeant.

You must be glad to see the closure of your service, the sergeant's wife, Jane, expresses on dry lips.

It is not the closure, Mis'ess Waddy. Only the ending of my tenure here. There is yet much reformation to be undertaken in the colony.

You have made this colony into a model of settlement, Sergeant Waddy fawns.

Cuthbertson turns and looks through the beads of rain upon the long window. There are dim lights on the hill. The lights are split like cat's eyes. They detain the night form of the penitentiary in their spotted chain, standing on the island's high outcrop.

I am sure you will agree, lieutenant, says James Scott, that without us industrious few, the wheel of civilisation would not turn.

Kelly clears his throat: The coal is shallow. The Huon pine does not regrow. The swans are extinct. The convicts are crooked. What truths we know here are truths to all the colony.

Cuthbertson wonders what Kelly means as his sight lays stranded on the dormitory, distantly represented by shots of bleared orange lantern light. He brings himself back to the room: With the aid of providence, Lieutenant Wright may not encounter the tribulations I have known in reforming this savage region of Van Diemen's Land. It is after progress that we run, Master Kelly. The coal may be in short supply, and the Huon may retreat deeper inland, but so long as there are prisoners, then by God let them have work. For now, it is to Hobart for me, and who knows after that.

Perhaps you'll join the war again, says Jane Waddy, raising a dark, Irish eyebrow.

Which war?

There is always a war for heroes, lieutenant.

I suppose. Let me say, if this is peace, I'd take Talavera any day. Cuthbertson is a little tipsy. He reaches for the ewer again.

The prisoners are often asking what that means, says Douglas. The name of Talavera.

Cuthbertson feels his breast pocket with his left hand. Softly he plucks an iron key. He strides to his desk in the adjacent bedchamber, unlocks the lowest drawer, and takes out an old pistol wrapped in scarlet cloth.

You were never a cavalryman, Waddy proclaims as Cuthbertson returns, an ancient dragoon's pistol in hand.

Cuthbertson pauses to think of the father he only knew in heirlooms and name, of Ireland, of wars before his time. It was my father's, he explains. I was told it was dead weight for an infantryman to carry in battle, many years ago ... at Porto, Douglas, when we first defeated the French. The battle of Talavera came after.

Cuthbertson holds the pistol with familiar assurance, a readiness in the springs of his hand that never leaves a king's man. The smell of the iron barrel is as steely as shed blood. That smell carries him away in time, to old and forgotten outposts, behind doors that can only be unlocked by that smell; the subtle impurity of gunpowder, the lifeless, burned perfume that climbs out of the scratches in the bore chamber, the stain of sweat against the stock. He can taste the spice and dull cold metal of powder and ball. To hold that weapon is to forget the years and remember one moment only. She is more than three pounds of dead weight.

Cuthbertson narrates his finest hour with rum in one hand and the old brown pistol in the other. He cuts crosses from wall to wall.

The Duke of Wellington led the army that night. We had been probing the French for weeks. We had won a battle at the town of Porto and given chase. They had finally retreated from Portugal, the dogs. We were in a ghastly valley somewhere south of Madrid when the French surprised us. We fought through the night. All night we vied for the hill.

Cuthbertson reaches in front of his face. He can see the hill.

At daybreak the sun came galloping over the lip of the valley, and the French tried us a final time. Wellington called for my regiment—the 48th. The brave 48th. We laid beneath the crest of the hill, and as the French climbed over we took to a charge, bayonets raised over our heads.

Cuthbertson lifts his glass. His nostrils widen for air.

The sky was blood at dawn. The pigs drove up the hill swearing in their filthy French. We rushed them with our bayonets.

Cuthbertson clutches his own garments.

I can still feel the resistance of enemy flesh on my blade. That is when I took up this pistol, surrounded by men with long muskets. I put down one, two with my bayonet, another with my hands. The fourth would have had me—I was a musket's reach from him—but he did not account for three pounds of dead weight.

Cuthbertson's guests twist in their places to behold the squalling weather outside.

By morning the French had quit. The bastards had left their wounded behind. So many were dead of our number. We had won Portugal, and Wellington was a hero. The finest soldier Britain ever produced.

Ireland, Jane Waddy says.

Pardon?

Ireland. The Duke of Wellington was born in Ireland.

Cuthbertson falls silent. Is an Irishman an Irishman in the British army? he asks, not desiring an answer.

Is this our empire, here at the end of the Earth? Sergeant Waddy speaks. Am I Scottish-born? Do I forget *where* I was born?

Would that I could, Cuthbertson despairs. He says out loud: An Irishman could not have defeated the French. He was England-trained.

I would have thought you were proud of your countryman, Jane Waddy probes.

A man of the army has no country, Cuthbertson claims.

Lucas proposes: If you were a sailor, you would know that a man of the sea must love his country. He must love it if he is to return to it, to return to land.

I thought a sailor has loyalty to the sea alone.

Loyalty? The sea is loyal to no one. If anything, a sailor hates the sea. Man is not meant to be at sea. It will betray him.

The storm upsets the conversation.

It will not be long till you are due to the sea, captain, concludes Kelly.

Captain? Too premature, Cuthbertson says through a smile he cannot fight.

You will no doubt be promoted, Douglas praises. Wright has your shoulders to stand on.

Cuthbertson strides to the window, pensive and proud.

Governor Sorell was a wise man sending you here, Kelly lays on. It is a shame that his government must cease the way it has. I wonder if Arthur …

Governor Sorell, Cuthbertson exclaims. His face is in the rain of the glass. Kelly makes an attempt to resume his thought but Cuthbertson cuts his voice again: The *Governor Sorell*. Douglas, do you see?

He beckons the clerk to the window and demands he look to the harbour. The sea is distended into a black waste of barrows which threaten to swallow the island. Waves grope the Huon schooner. The *Governor Sorell*, the first ship built at Settlement Island, is seduced from its moorings.

Gentlemen, Mis'ess Waddy, apologies, Cuthbertson smooths

his red coat. Douglas, with me. Where is Smith?

Where are you going? Kelly is disturbed.

The schooner, says Cuthbertson as he collects his effects. He fastens the strap of his varnished shako under his chin. My *Governor Sorell*. She is dragging in the storm.

Douglas has dashed into the rain. Shortly a bell rings in the hurly-burly.

Let me come with you then, Kelly volunteers.

No need, Cuthbertson cuts the mariner back. He brings his greatcoat, like a great fold of elephant hide, to his shoulders. He enjoys the brief reflection of his tall grey body in the long mirror. He slides his fingers between the buttons of his coat, as the generals did in Portugal. The brass badge of his shako boasts the arms of the 48th. TALAVERA. Pour another rum, he says, unable to prise his pupils from the mirror. I will return when the boat is secured.

Cuthbertson leaves his quarters behind. Douglas rejoins him with the coxswain Smith. The wind hurls javelins of sand and mud in the furious spray. The sea stinks in the dark air, but Cuthbertson knows his way to the dock blindfolded; he does not need the aid offered up by faint scars of lightning.

Put out the whaler, Cuthbertson orders Smith. From the jetty he strains the pale strakes of the schooner from the night, drifting sou'east towards the river mouth. Ready all the boats.

Let her wreck, Smith pleads. We'll drown saving her.

Cuthbertson shelters his eyes from the rain. He chases the phantom colour of the schooner until it disappears into the darkness. He named her in honour of the governor who gave him his post. Sorell is due to depart the colony in March. By that time Cuthbertson will be a captain, and he will return to Hobart with a choice gift in the Huon schooner. He will not let her wreck.

Where is your courage? he snaps. Cuthbertson is the first to step onto the trembling whaleboat. Eight to the oars! he commands.

The frigid sea beats the ribs of the boat without mercy. It leads others towards the fallow speck on the night's edge. Cuthbertson growls at the oarsmen. The sinuous paddles warp in the stress of the waves. The lights of Settlement Island vanish behind them.

Although his fingers are numb, Cuthbertson's throat is hot with a coating of rum. Surrounded by high mountains of water, he thinks of the songs they used to sing in the ranks of the 48th. He returns to the bayonet charge at Talavera.

Row! he bellows.

In the flash of lightning Cuthbertson sees Wellington upon a horse, charging Portuguese fields. Cuthbertson glimpses the approaching shore in vagaries of lightning. The river draws near.

The schooner skitters on the foaming sea like a wild horse corralled. He thinks of her gargantuan worth on the market, the vindication of Macquarie Harbour – all the toil of this place is held inside her layered planks, her Huon mast, her impervious hull. Without her, it has all been for nothing.

The ship is in the jaws of the river now. They cross into the perilous currents of the harbour's narrow end.

Follow the squall! Cuthbertson gathers the voice of Smith in the storm.

The whaleboat edges near to the schooner and clashes oar to hull. Smith stumbles to the portside. He reaches for the flailing ropes. His hand retrieves a line. The other sailors throw hooks over the gunwale. Smith leaps aboard and slides to the anchor. It is cast overboard. The schooner lurches as it bites the bottom. Cuthbertson watches Smith fall on his back.

The *Governor Sorell* surrenders, exceeded by the waves. The sailors pull off their hooks. Smith returns aboard. They are encircled by the other ships.

Cuthbertson stands on the starboard.

Lieutenant, he hears the sound of distant pleading but is captivated by the snared boat. Lieutenant. It is Smith fretting. We should make back.

Cuthbertson touches his shako, the brass badge emblazoned TALAVERA. The wind tries to thieve it from him, just as the sea strained to drown his schooner. He has defeated the wind. He has defeated the sea. In seven hundred and twenty-seven nights, he has bettered the scum in his charge, the convicts – Alexander Pearce – he has beaten them. And the ghastly gates of hell, not even they could foreshorten his fate. His captaincy waits. Surely it waits. His life has been a bayonet charge. God's favour falls on the bold, the tireless, and he is such a man.

The whaler is turned and rowed back through the persecution of the water. The wind is against them. They dip into the treacherous currents of the river mouth.

Wave! Smith cries.

Forward! Cuthbertson gives his order.

Sir. Smith is frantic.

Forward! Cuthbertson bleats through the sting of ocean spray. Forward. The ocean swells. Cuthbertson stands rampant in the bow of the whaleboat. He does not look to see Smith call to brace for a rogue wave.

Lieutenant!

Cuthbertson is blinded by water. When his eyes repair, he sees the boat fill with a lightless black liquid. Its starboard disappears. The portside rises.

Wave!

The moon vanishes behind the rolling hull. The rising vessel groans and crashes down. Shouts are doused in the petrifying water. Cuthbertson gasps. The sheet of air between his mouth and the boat thins too quickly.

Then a hand from above grasps the sleeve of his greatcoat. Cuthbertson tries to grip the fingers. He has lost his sight. All the breath in his nose is gone too. He can only feel the light numb sensation of a desperate grip. The fingers are in his palm. He holds them in one hand as tight as his numb hand will allow, and reaches up with the other, but the foreign hand loses purchase.

Sorell's brass plate cuts into his throat. He feels the sudden weight of his apparel. Dead weight. It is dragging him down.

PEARCE

Hobart-town, June 1824 A.D.

Alexander's cell beneath the sandy ground of Hobart-town is larger than his sitting space was on the *Duke of York*. But his shrivelled legs in bands of iron remember too well the journey to Macquarie Harbour. He recalls sitting beside Dalton who spoke in haughty tones. Dalton is dead now.

Dalton deserved what he got. He had betrayed his own kind. He had flogged another for fear of his own back. He had been the one to lose more skin in the end.

Alexander's crime is a great joke in Hobart-town gaol but he cannot see the humour. They all shared the moral wound in the wilderness, they all took pieces of Dalton, but none of them joked. They reconciled what they had done, and agreed that God had left them behind. They cursed Dalton after the deed – he deserved death if nothing else – but they did not speak a light word about the act. It was unspoken even in the wilderness.

A rising bell. It must be the hour, or a marriage, or a burial.

It is a burial which Alexander waits for, sitting in irons awaiting death at the end of a noose – a loose end tied up in a knot. He awaits his hanging and a shallow, nameless grave. But before then, he awaits a visitor.

His redemption is a false promise. If the government has decided his life is forfeit, why would God disagree? Who can save his soul? Yet the gaol keeper John Bisdee tells him that the Reverend Mister Phillip Conolly will try.

Ballinamuck, says Alexander.

He has not met a man of his native country which he likes. Tommy Caldwell's face is disfigured by decaying memory. If he had liked *him*, their friendship is soured by all the others.

He's a countryman of yours, says Bisdee as if Monaghan is a font of fond memories for Alexander. That must be comforting for you.

Every Irishman I ever known has been a bastard. Alexander glances at the black film of water in a groove on the ground. He sees his own dark eyes.

You're an Irishman.

Every Irishman, Alexander repeats.

There is the clatter of opening and closing doors in the gaol house beyond the stairwell. Alexander straightens his back. Bisdee disappears from view. When he returns to the barred threshold of Alexander's cell he is not alone. The gaoler pulls a stool.

You may sit here, reverend. Bisdee sets the stool in the corridor.

Alexander peers through the bars at a pewter crucifix, silver against a plain black robe. Of course he will sit behind bars.

Please, John. I'll not sit this side of the bars. Be handy with the keys. I would meet Alexander the man. Conolly collects the stool in his arm. Alexander is suspicious.

The gaoler has now left Alexander with Conolly's discerning grey eyes. We meet in the third act, Pearce. But it is not too late, Conolly says to him. His eyes are stony but there is nothing cold about them. His mouth is quick and dry, and though he does not smile, the crow's-feet in his eyes smirk. He puts down the stool as a milkmaid does.

Aren't we two boys far from home, the priest says with a muddled sad nostalgia. He speaks in Irish. Alexander's suspicion grows. He feels the cover of Conolly's eyes, but for the first time since his trial it does not dowse him in loathing. I want to make sense of what happened to you, Pearce, says Conolly.

I have been sentenced to death.

Not what sentence you've been given—what *happened* to you.

Alexander winces.

You got palsy on the left arm there?

Palsy?

Yea, palsy, yea.

Alexander plunges his unclean finger nails into the muscle to revive it. I just been sitting here a while, is all.

Would you like to go for a walk? I am sure I could convince Bisdee to let us free for an hour.

You are not half bad for an Irishman. Alexander does not expect to say it. Every Irishman I ever known has been a bastard.

You're an Irishman.

So people keep telling me.

Conolly's voice rings out to Bisdee who returns flushed and panting from the physical strain of mounting the stair only to descend again. Conolly speaks with friendly authority and convinces Bisdee to give them an hour in the air, provided Alexander walks in his chains.

Alexander has forgotten what the strain of blood in his hams feels like. It is a tragic loss. He needs support from Conolly as they round the gaol house corner to be away from the eyes of other prisoners.

Did you ever meet Lieutenant Cuthbertson? Alexander asks, thinking of all the Irish tyrants he has ever known. Dalton and uncle Adam were bad, but Cuthbertson was worst in his mind.

Not proper, says Conolly.

Alexander cannot keep his mouth from curling. He is dead, he exclaims. The bastard drowned. By the living Jingo, if you want to know the mind of God, think of that. For so long I thought God on the side of tyrants. He paid no mind while John Ollery was flogged to death. Then he drowned Jack Robertson. If you want to know the mind of God, you cannot.

Conolly twists his face. Why Sorell gave that man his own island, I will never know, but you are not meet to blow the sawdust in his eyes, Alexander. You know what log there is in yours.

You do not understand. We would never have run if living was not as poor as it was.

And were circumstances not as poor on Scattergood's run? Were they not as poor in the road-gang?

Alexander is silent, discomforted by Conolly's familiarity with his past.

You're a bolter, Alexander.

Alexander remembers Saunders tricking him into thinking life was easy on the lam. It was easy as far as the bolter knew, easy on the charts of grog and liberty. But that life was hard on the charts of health and happiness. Alexander is ruined by the polluting memory of Saunders inside him. At least Saunders is dead like Dalton.

You're a bolter, Conolly repeats. Alexander is silent for a long time while he thinks of the day Cuthbertson arrested him for forgery. How he should have bolted then.

No man deserves a cage, he says at last.

The sharp laugh these words draw out of Conolly hurts Alexander. His voice fills the empty yard where they loiter: So men say who would prefer no rule of law, no chains whatsoever. Well, you're in a cage now, Alexander. And it is one you cannot flee from.

If I had my choice of islands I would have stayed on Spike, Alexander mithers. Do away with Van Diemen's Land and Sarah Island. We were treated so small in Macquarie Harbour. It was a breaking every day.

It was for the good of your soul, says Conolly.

Alexander does not answer Conolly's words, which he hates for their utter falsity. He only screams and then begins to sob. The gaol wall hurls back his agonised cry.

Conolly looks quickly about but they are alone. He lowers his voice: We will always grasp for the fates we might have had. That is because the current is so dire. But you needn't fear God's judgement if you are absolved in life. That is why I have come. I know what has become of your resolve, but there is still work you may do to salvage eternity. Do not cast eternity away like a soiled rag.

What brought *you* to Van Diemen's Land? Alexander asks to get away from Conolly's preaching. He is not sure the priest is a decent man anymore.

Conolly sighs: I heard there was freedom from persecution here.

It is now Alexander's turn to laugh. It is a mottled laugh that draws lingering tears from his eyes. Conolly talks a little further, but with sympathy.

Ireland is still in pain. I had no family there, and the prospect of seeing the new world enticed me. We all err, Alexander. And then it is too late, and we must live with the decisions we've made—what's more, we must face them and not be afraid of what we are.

Alexander is tired of walking so he sits in the sand. He asks a question: If I confess sins on Monday, but sin again on Wednesday, and then confess on Friday, do I still carry the weight of Monday's sin?

Conolly thinks a little and then answers, No.

Then why I am punished again and again for things I done so long ago. I mean my thieving.

It was thieving what brought your here, was it?

Aye. That first crime opened up all the rest. I was in a bad way in Monaghan.

And I suppose being in a bad way gives us the right to suspend criminal law?

Tell: would you rob if you were hungry?

Conolly has been asked this before because he answers very quickly: Do not ask me that. Ask me instead if I would like it if I were robbed.

Well, would you?

I know the bible tells me that if I am struck on the cheek to turn the other, but it also says stealing is a crime, so I will say: hit me on the cheek and I will not sue, but steal my best Sunday shirt and I will prosecute with the bible in my hand. One cannot disagree with the bible, after all.

Famous, says Alexander. I thought there might be a way around it.

Remember that there were two thieves crucified with our Lord. Do you think the moaning thief got the same treatment as the penitent one?

They were both crucified, were they not?

Yes, but one went to heaven and the other hell, all because the moaner wanted proof of Jesus's divinity.

Alexander says it seems an awfully petty thing to do, for Jesus to damn the moaning thief because he asked for a miracle: Do we not ask for miracles all the time?

Conolly tells him he is being peevish.

Alexander says he is not being peevish. He says if a child asks their teacher why a word should be spelled so, and they are struck, but another child says, Remember me, if I spell this wrong, and gets kissed, then the teacher is a fiend.

You're walking away from your question, Alexander. Theft is a venial sin. It can be forgiven on Monday. If you murder a man or eat a man on Wednesday, that can also be forgiven on Friday, but you may be hanged for it on Saturday.

Alexander hangs his head.

You know the difference, Conolly says. Venial sins hurt your relationship with God. Mortal sins break it entirely. But your eternal salvation and the law of this world are two different things.

Would I have been better in the eyes of God if I died? Alexander asks.

Conolly cannot answer.

Alexander goes on, feeling petulant: The penalty for what I done is death, but if I did not do what I done, hunger would have killed me. Does this mean I was doomed either way?

You were not doomed until you made a choice, says Conolly. And you will not get any closer to God while you dance around blaming everyone but yourself. If you confess, you can be with God, but that does not absolve you from paying the price in this life.

Alexander goes quiet, thinking of sin, sin, sin. He wonders what is the difference between venial and mortal sins if he can confess both of them away in the same sitting.

What about being Irish? he asks. When everything else is confessed, I cannot confess that away, can I? Or being catholic.

That last one is an irony. You are doing a famous job of avoiding your past, Alexander. I want you to tell me about Sarah Island.

Alexander would rather not. He has been back twice, and the third journey of mind wounds him in a different way. They retrace the path to the cells to give Alexander time to order his thoughts. When they are back in Alexander's cell, feeling that he can no longer evade the priest's piercing mind, Alexander unwinds his last two years in reverse.

He tells Conolly that young Thomas Cox convinced him to escape with a lie, and that when he discovered the boy could not swim he feared he would be killed, for Cox was strong in his youth and had not seen as many floggings as Alexander. So he killed him only to protect his life and went his own way after. But he was so overcome with guilt that he returned to the shore to see that Cox would be buried. When Cuthbertson retrieved him, being such a fast talker and Alexander simple, he was not able to explain the truth of it, and Cuthbertson, desiring to be rid of him, said proudly in front of witnesses that Alexander had murdered – he would not hear another word of it, because he wanted to be rid of Alexander.

Are you saying Cuthbertson invented Cox's mutilated body,

are you? Conolly interrupts.

Alexander sits in silence.

Conolly allows him to retrieve the events of his first escape from Sarah Island, but stops him to ask about Kennerly and Brown.

You must tell me why you confessed the whole thing to Reverend Knopwood in court. I am curious. Are you really so honest a man, Pearce?

Dead men tell no tales, says Alexander with flat recital. I did not tell Knopwood the truth because I am a good man. There have been many times I wanted to be dead – Alexander draws the scenes across his mind but does not voice them: after Greenhill when he could not find his way, when uncle Adam put his hand on his mouth, at his father's burial, Joseph Saunders, the shit and piss of the journey from Ireland – but for small reasons none of them had killed me. So when it came to it, I thought, why die now? I already been through so much, it would be a waste of my own flesh to die.

Kennerly and Brown escaped us. I honestly thought they had told Cuthbertson about the deed and Cuthbertson the governor, and that I was surely damned. The whole colony would know what we did. So I think to myself: they know what you done Pearce, do not lie about it, but tell them it was not your fault, tell them it was Greenhill's. That way you will not hang.

Conolly rubs his face aggressively with two hands: Jesus and Mary, lies and more lies.

Alexander scowls: I mean that it was Greenhill's fault the first time, it was. He feels his own scowl melt upon his face into a facial shrug. I discovered too late that Kennerly and Brown had died before telling anyone about us. If I had have known, I would not have said a word. I would not be here.

It is a lie that would keep you alive, then, Conolly elaborates. But God would know.

I figured I was damned in the future state anyway. At least I could enjoy life a little longer.

You are mistaken about one thing, Alexander: Knopwood didn't believe you and he sent you back regardless. You were always going to try escape again, whether you lied or no, and if that is the logic, you were always going to murder Cox and pay for the crime this way.

So it is fate, then.

Conolly is wordless for a while. He goes so long without answering that the notion of fate vanishes. Instead he says, Do you still believe you are innocent?

Of Cox, no. Of everyone else, yes.

I cannot absolve you of your sins unless you confess it all. Only a priest has the power to absolve sin. Conolly's eyes suddenly look far away. I am more powerful than a saint, Alexander. Through me, you might not suffer in the life to come.

Good for you. No priest kept me from suffering in this life. Alexander smiles. Now he sobs. His expression irritates Conolly's countenance, being crying eyes and a gleeful jaw bearing rotten teeth in disagreement with his tears.

Conolly ignores the insult: You say you do not want to die, Alexander. I want to know, why didn't you go on after Cox? Why did you return, when you must have known you would pay with your life?

Alexander cannot answer because he does not know. He tries some stories but Conolly pulverises them.

Not a modicum of guilt, says Conolly, shaking his head. Lie to all other men, but if you lie to me there will be no salvation for you. The priest opens his bible and reads from it: Whose soever sins ye remit, they are remitted unto them; and whose soever sins ye retain, they are retained. Do not carry the burden alone.

These words are spoken softly as Conolly rises and makes away. Alexander feels like each echoed step is the drifting particles of salvation wafting away from the beaten rug of his life. Conolly reaches the gate and patiently awaits Bisdee with the keys. Raking his back with eyes, Alexander calls out.

I was broke by hunger. I did not want to journey alone. The first time I had Greenhill to the very end. I did not know how far any town was. I started to feel the chill again. So I returned and had a mind to tell them Cox was drowned. I thought I could escape punishment and they would only give me 25 lashes for absconding. But I forgot the piece of Cox in my pocket. I told them it was only proof of his death but Cuthbertson did not believe me. I was damned by that piece of Cox.

Conolly turns his grievous face to Alexander with an expression of perplexity. Bisdee arrives and the gate opens and shuts. Conolly's faces is now broken into strips by the bars, but its eyes are horribly sad. Alexander has told him the truth, so why does he look in pain?

Pray for contrition, Alexander, he says in a long and tired voice.

I do not know how.

Conolly gives a final impressive flash of his eyes, brows heavy with anguish, but he does not say anything loud, only a whisper, little more than a breath with hurried words in Irish: *Neither do I.* Then Bisdee locks the gate and Conolly is gone.

CONOLLY

Hobart-town, July 1824 A.D.

The time has come, Pearce.

The locking gate punctuates Phillip's voice. Alexander is a lump of curdled milk against the dark stains of the cell wall. His gaunt face is retrieved from the shadows by a pale shaft which creeps down from the small high window. Alexander seems to be listening to the feet of the people in the gaol-yard and Macquarie-street above him. Phillip sets his bible on a stool at the intangible edge of the prisoner's ulcerous odour.

Phillip sees old John Terry in Alexander's rigid jaw, his wispy brown hair with long flanks. Alexander's nose is sharp and high like a piglet's but there is still John Terry about him. His cheeks are caved by rations and his lips are fastened tight. Phillip supposes any man would look the same who has passed through hell. Have you slept? he asks in Irish.

Alexander knuckles crusted eyes for an answer. His face is ossified. In the weeks since their first meeting, Phillip has visited a dozen times. He thinks their Irish conversation a bath of milk which has softened Alexander – Phillip has always thought his native language in possession of magic. So he invokes it for one more miracle: today is the eve of execution and Alexander has not yet confessed.

Phillip has not slept either. He has been searching for words in the small hours, words which might save Alexander today. In times before, he has been nothing but two ears to condemned men. Men normally open their mouths to empty their hearts the day before eternity, making hymns out of their final thoughts in voices that the world will never know again. They speak to know themselves.

Phillip may be a mantelpiece in those confessions, but he does not care; whatever provides the condemned with peace; that there may be solace in which God dwells – that is best for them; and if they remain genial upon the hanging stage, then Phillip's employers are satisfied. But Alexander worries Phillip.

Some days he seems oblivious to the steep drop which rends his path ahead. On others he is wistfully lost in his own excrement. Yesterday he was severe and abusive. Phillip supposes that is because yesterday he was told they had set the day for his hanging – he will not see the sun go down on Monday.

Two days does not afford much time to prepare for eternity. Phillip does not know any better than Alexander whether death is a thing he is ready for.

Phillip picks up his bible and sits on the stool.

Do you think God hears any of our prayers? Prisoners, I mean.

God hears all prayers, Phillip says with conviction.

Does He answer the prayers of a criminal?

The prayer is different from the man, Alexander. God does not turn a deaf ear to one man because of his stature. He hears and judges all prayers equally.

What of all men? Are we all judged equally? Alexander's voice is throaty as he speaks.

Blood must expiate blood, Phillip intones the law. It has been that way since the days of Moses. No amount of praying can change the law. Phillip wonders in himself if that is true, but now is not the moment to discuss doubts with Alexander Pearce. How do you feel? he asks, a little insincerely.

Afraid, is the only word on Alexander's lips. Can hell be any worse than what I been through?

Do not tempt damnation. Where you go from here is not for me to know, Phillip speaks up. I can only open the door. The way is for you to walk.

Alexander rubs weary eyes. Now he pinches his calves.

When did you last walk in the yard? Phillip asks with an eye on Alexander's whittled legs. For perhaps the last time, Phillip enlists Bisdee's sympathies and helps Alexander up the stairs.

As Alexander limps on Phillip's arm, he mutters a question: I wonder, reverend, how did you keep out of it? How did you keep free of the gutter when you were young?

God, says Phillip quickly, unable to ignore the pitiable memory of his sister's weathered face.

God rejected me, Alexander says. Phillip does not know if he should answer it as a question.

It is man who chooses God, Alexander, not the other way around. That is what you must do now, choose righteousness. The poverty of childhood is not to be lamented now. Whatever sins came with your home in county Monaghan, they are long distant. God is only concerned with your present state.

They come out into the quiet night yard. The angles of the stone wall enclose a gravel flat. Seabirds lark in the deep lightless clouds above them.

Do you remember Ballinamuck? Alexander asks.

Phillip does not speak. He recalls women he knew made widows by that battle. He dwells on the year whose numbers are black in every Irish memory. Then he turns his mind to his own condition. He counts himself fortunate amongst a race so poor. He knows he does not need to extol a criminal to see what has created a catholic Irishman like Alexander Pearce.

Alexander speaks of Ballinamuck with a cut tongue, the redcoat forever a bloodstain. How he must have hated a traitor of kind like Cuthbertson, Phillip thinks, an Irishman dressed in the colours of the royalists who fell upon Ballinamuck and killed so many of Ireland's poor. Phillip expects he has every reason to speak out upon the gallows, but as he looks in Alexander's dour face, he knows in his heart he will not.

The sight of his dejection brings to mind the governor's commission: he must walk the stage in silence. He is to be the first man executed by the new court, thinks Phillip. He is an example. Suddenly, Phillip is not afraid of the prisoner's fits of anger. He knows Alexander is not the kind of man who will stand at the gates of eternity and use his numbered breaths to curse God.

Some do, but not for Alexander. Phillip now understands, though he cannot trace the footsteps of the thought, that the same attribute which bought him his survival is what will silence him in the end: Alexander is a coward.

He followed seven men into the savage wilderness, and only when all but one had fallen did he muster the courage to slay the navigator who had led him through – and only in his sleep. Phillip was repulsed by the thought. Even his second escape was not encouraged by vigour. He could only escape once Cox had done the work.

Cox had gathered the hooks and tinder and rations. And what pushed him over the edge? The risk of another lashing for a crime he did not commit. Even when he killed Cox, he did not have the means to kill him standing, nor did he have the courage to run. He would rather suffer at Sarah Island, in the company of other sufferers, than face it all alone, than face what he had become.

Phillip thinks that Macquarie Harbour has achieved that which is was designed to do – his thought is stalled when Alexander speaks unexpected.

Saint Bríd's cross is upside down.

The prisoner's head is fallen back, his bulging throat sticking out. Alexander lifts a hand in explanation.

My mother always told me those stars were saint Bríd's cross.

Phillip finds the stars of the constellation crux after some time. What Alexander calls saint Bríd's is only a southern cross in the Van Diemen's Land sky.

My mother's name is Bríd, says Alexander without weeping. When my father was killed, my mother took up the rushes on our floor and wove a star out of them. She told me it were the cross of a saint. She showed me where the stars were in the sky. She told me those stars would always protect me.

Alexander spits on the ground. The bitch did not even say goodbye when I went away. He wanders in a circle and then pulls something out of his pocket. He looks longingly at the object in his hand before speaking: The saints do not care about us.

I didn't tell you about my father, Phillip says. He draws closer to Alexander. Whatever is in the prisoner's hand, he closes his fingers to conceal it. My father was a priest of sorts. He belonged to an order. I did not know when I was a young boy that priests could not have children, for my father had many children with many different women. I only grew up in a house with my older sister, Nora. Our neighbours called us Martin Conolly's *relatives,* but they all knew. When the rising happened, my father disappeared. We never knew if he fought and died or if he just went into hiding. If he hid we did not know who from—he was a sinner in both camps. I was sent to St Patrick's College. My sister paid for me to be there with her hands. She worked herself into an early grave, and I never thanked her for it.

Phillip clears his throat: My father told me one thing of the saints that has stayed with me. I named the chapel here in Hobart after one of them. Have you ever heard of Virgil? He is the patron saint of all the Irish, more especially the far-flung Irish. I've not known many churches named for him. I suppose that isn't much of a surprise. Those still living in Ireland and Europe have little need of a saint who cares for the wayward traveller. They still know the feeling of home. They've not had to try plant roots in hungry soil. My father told me that Virgil believed in a round Earth long before we sent ships west to find out. He went further than those who simply claimed the world had another side. He claimed that people lived there. In him God has given us a relative to pray to, someone who knew that there must have been a darker side to the world, and that one day we would know the displeasure of living on it.

Alexander's face is turned away. Phillip cannot tell if he is listening. He thinks of his sister and his father and saint Virgil. He thinks of unanswered prayers that he has made to the saint of a lost people in his own life. Then he sizes Alexander from head to foot and chocks up saliva in his mouth: Fuck the deaf saints. He spits.

Alexander looks at him now.

The saints didn't die for you, and you're not going to die for them. There's only one who matters. He that heareth my word and believeth on Him that sent me, hath everlasting life, and shall not come into condemnation; but is passed from death unto life.

Alexander says nothing but appears intrigued. Phillip offers a hand. Come Pearce, I have bread and wine in your cell.

The night air, like Irish words, has done something to the composition of Alexander's parts. Phillip fans the pages of his bible. He preaches from it.

Knowing this, that our old man is crucified with Him, that the body of sin might be destroyed, that henceforth we should not serve sin. For he that is dead is freed from sin.

Phillip perceives a light flicker in Alexander's dull eyes.

Now if we be dead with Christ, we believe that we shall also live with Him: knowing that Christ being raised from the dead dieth no more; death hath no more dominion over Him.

Alexander bobs his grim head as though in understanding. Understanding is knowing that he can die into life, thinks Phillip, as Jesus had; that by the stripes of the Saviour he is permitted everlasting life if he will but confess. Phillip kneels to explain these things, then he reads again. He has the bible parted between two fingers.

Repent ye therefore, and be converted, that your sins may be blotted out, when the times of refreshing shall come from the presence of the Lord. For *all* have sinned, and come short of the glory of God; being justified freely by his grace through the redemption that is in Christ Jesus. For whosoever shall call upon the name of the Lord shall be saved.

Alexander rubs his frail legs in anguish and speaks: What must I do?

Confess, Alexander. Let God hear your sins.

I have killed. I have murdered, he says suddenly. He puts a

hand upon his mouth and murmurs, I have been buggered by and eaten ... bejesus. His eyes press together. I have thieved and lied. I am a sinner.

Phillip sits with Alexander. Repent this prayer with me, he says. He goes on with words he has taught so many fearful people, and when Alexander has finished following him, they say together: Amen.

May the passion of our Lord Jesus Christ and the intercession of the blessed virgin Mary heal your sins and reward you with eternal life. Alexander Pearce, I absolve you in the name of the Father, the Son and the Holy Ghost.

When he has finished speaking Phillip produces a ewer of sour wine and a plate of crumbs. He gives Alexander a wafer and takes one himself, chanting as Alexander places the bread on his tongue: This is the body of Christ which was given up for you.

He passes the wine which Alexander drinks eagerly: And this is the blood that was shed for you.

The eucharist has finished and Phillip, feeling a moment of weariness, scoops up his stool. I will leave you to your own prayers now, Alexander, he says. You should be vigilant tonight, but don't forget to sleep. And don't forget to shave. You look abominable. I will see you at first light. He steps away and raps on the gate. Bisdee has not arrived when he is fearfully turned by a shout which fills the cell.

Reverend! Conolly! Pearce is crawling along the ground. Phillip presses his back into the bars. He can hear Bisdee's footfalls only faintly at the highest stair. Alexander crawls right up to him. His legs must be dreadfully weak because he does not stand, only lies upon his stomach and snaps his neck up at the priest.

You must take this from me. His hand is outstretched. A small white brooch sits upon his palm. His eyes do not sink from their desperation until Phillip takes it. It looks like a loaf of bread. There are letters on the side of it. Phillip is about to remark when Bisdee startles him at the gate. He startles Alexander as well, who scratches his way back to the wall. Phillip buries the brooch in his pocket and leaves Alexander behind.

CONOLLY

Hobart-town, July 1824 A.D.

Phillip leaves the gaol with a heavy head. Though weary from his labours, he is filled with a foolish, tired urge to walk down Hobart's broad street instead of uphill to St Virgil's.

He looks in the direction of the rivulet. The dark shapes of the prisoners' houses huddle against the reedy banks. Phillip clutches his bible close and drags his feet down the hill.

He imagines the figure of a woman, her hands rough and calloused, her face speckled with sores and cuts, but with shamrock eyes that cannot be defeated. He wishes to see that face again, but he knows even if she opens her door to him, her green eyes will not be the same. Even as he sucks sourly on his regrets, he asks himself when her light had been dimmed. He wonders if her fate might change.

He is supposed to be a bridge between the worlds of prisoner and free, but he feels as though his cleats have fallen through. Even Alexander's confession does not resuscitate his crestfallen heart.

He knows something of the pain of prison, but the mind of Johanna Lynch escapes him. Is it truly worse to live under a priest's roof than the roof of an uncaring man? Are the things he cannot offer – carnal love and lavish, albeit fleeting, tastes – poorer than his gifts of safe harbour and steady care? Is he so blinded by a puritan's cataracts that he cannot see his own fatal flaw? He wants to know why Johanna remains on the other side of the water, persisting in her wind-battered hovel, plagued by hungry children, and abused by a hard, unfeeling man.

He recalls his spat with Sophia Nightingale. She had forced him to entertain John Hellings, which Phillip did for no other reason but his love for Sophia and her child. Phillip had seen Hellings drunk in the street so many times; there was no use in warning her again and again. It would not make her see his way, just as he would not see hers. Perhaps she knew his vices and simply did not care.

If Johanna does not care for the sins of a prisoner like John Cavanagh then she is a fool. It risks the ruin of her children. Phillip pauses as he comes to a shallow sandy ford in the rivulet. He looks into the east where his feet point to the lumps of horizon smeared with rosehips. He can make a cannibal come with him to the gallows, but he cannot make a woman follow him.

Phillip grinds away his time in waiting on the cart-track outside Johanna Lynch's sod-roofed hut. He lets darkness fall over him. The western sky turns from pink reflections of the east's bloodshed to a sky stained with gunpowder. A far-off red star glints in the deep. Phillip cannot tell if John Cavanagh is home.

He is not afraid of the prisoner. He does not think a servant of the crown would harm him, even in such a place. Even they are wary of God's priesthood, if not faithful in their devotions. He is worried for Johanna. He fears what might become of her if Cavanagh thinks she has a suitor.

An hour goes by before Phillip hears a young child's voice break into crying in the bark hut. Johanna's cooing voice pricks an awful delight in his heart. There is no man's voice beside it.

He draws nearer to the door but is arrested by Johanna's speech: Phillip, she says without emotion. She is looking at him between gathered curtains.

May I come in? Phillip asks abruptly through the window.

After a few unspoken moments Johanna appears in the door with an infant on her arm, sucking on a bone coral and half asleep. She closes the door behind her and takes a few steps outside.

John is sleeping, she warns. Brigid as well.

Phillip tries not to look at her swollen belly covered in thin muslin. He can see red nipples hanging low behind her dress.

Do not ask me about the pregnancy, she says in a manner which disarms Phillip.

How? is the only word he can summon.

Johanna's look is customary: Need I explain where babies come from, reverend?

Phillip must devote thought to closing his mouth.

Johanna's eyes suddenly darken: I am sorry about Mary Ann. I saw Sophia about a month ago. No mother should—I know the pain I would feel were it my own child.

She was not my daughter, Phillip apologises, feeling suddenly foolish.

You do not have to say that, Phillip. I know you cared for the girl.

How is Brigid? Phillip asks, remembering when he had christened her in the waters of the creek.

Johanna affords half a smile. She is a little wretch. She speaks for herself now. I thought the crying was over when she started speaking, but she cries and cries. John cannot stand it.

How is John?

Johanna draws her eyes to slits. Her dark brows come to rest in straight lines. Shall we ask each other how each of our close friends and relations are to pass the time? She shifts her child from one hip to the other. How come you are here?

Because I have not been. I should have come, but I have been distracted.

Johanna hums: Alexander Pearce.

He confessed tonight. Phillip cannot scrub the gloat off his words. He could never speak of this to Sophia. He confessed, Johanna. She looks troubled. Phillip listens to his own voice, which sounds to him too much like a child, so he lowers it an octave: It has taken weeks but I have finally reached the day, and not a day too late.

Is that why you came here? Johanna asks. Because the

wretched Irish cannibal reminds you of a wretched Irish whore?

Phillip draws a breath but is cut off before he can defend himself. Johanna is laughing.

Relax, Phillip. It was a joke. Tell me, did he understand when you took communion that by flesh you actually meant bread?

Phillip stamps his foot. A moment of good humour boils away. Johanna rebukes him with a shoosh, flicking her wary eyes to the bedroom window, but Phillip must expel his anger.

I thought you would be better, of all people, says Phillip unable to resist. Knopwood, the governor—everybody laughs. I think it is a shield drawn up from the deepest pit in us. I have heard men speak of him as though he is a monster who packed his friends for lunch. And here you go with another joke to distance yourself from him. We do not want to explain what he did, and yet I am supposed to explain it well enough to extract his confession, to save his soul. Does anyone want him saved?

Johanna is wrathful. He does not deserve it, she sneers. She may not believe this, but believe it or not she must know how it hurts Phillip.

Easy to say, Phillip grumbles, checking his sound. Easy to forget that there is a man who, beaten to his extremity, escaped in a band of eight and was made to survive by the foulest means. Easy to say: not I. I would never do such a thing. You know Ireland as well as I, Johanna. You know what it has made us. You do not know Sarah Island. Imagine being sent out of there and into a chasm with only bread baked to rot. But it is not hell. It is our own island.

My, you *have* been distracted. Johanna shows her teeth in a smile. Her glaring green eyes cannot offend Phillip, no matter how haughty they are. Her wit almost makes him laugh at his own piety.

He has cooled. He sends a quick eye to the door to ensure his shouts have not roused Cavanagh.

It is no excuse, he says. The way we left matters, the way that I left you, it was poorly. I have thought of you often.

Thoughts without actions are no better than air, Johanna says idly. Although, I do appreciate you coming.

Phillip sits in a bug-bitten silence. I wanted to know, he begins again, if you will be attending the hanging tomorrow?

Likely I will.

Don't, Phillip says curtly. The colony would be a fairer place if fewer people were obsessed with the living and dying of others.

Are you not obsessed with the living of others?

I believe that is my work.

Do not be so obsessed with living as to forget how to live, Phillip.

I will try. Phillip feels Johanna slipping away from him. Are you well?

Phillip, I really must feed my baby, and I am certain you do not want me pulling up this muslin with you about. And the child is being eaten half to death. Will you call again? Her brows slant with sincerity.

Phillip smiles. Why don't you call at St Virgil's?

Johanna's laugh is stunted. A woman of my *occupation* calling at a priest's door might raise talk in town. You may wish for folk to be less concerned with the doings of others, but I am afraid it will never be that way.

Phillip chafes. He chokes on a thought: If a prostitute visited a priest, would the town gossips call her penitent or would they call him promiscuous?

You do not need to let what happened on the *Janus* chart the rest of your life, Phillip offers.

Johanna's eyes light up in genuine rage. That is rich coming from a virgin on a government pension. Do I let it chart my life, reverend, or has it charted yours? Alexander Pearce may be the first real worry of your life.

Phillip bites back: Is that what you think of my occupation? Try carrying a dozen consciences along with your own.

O! but I do – the bodies of paying men mean nothing to me. It is their consciences I dread. Do not talk to me, I say, please do anything but talk to me. But they talk to me, maybe because they have had their fill of priests who want to hear confessions.

O! Sad, Phillip snipes. They must have heavy consciences, these men you lie with. Did John Terry have a heavy conscience, did he?

Johanna slams the door.

Phillip stands alone with his black sleeves by his side, his bible pressed uselessly under his arm. He will never take her with him now.

He turns his feet to the path again, and is bitterly reminded that he has not made confession once in three years. He has confessed to God and to himself, but without another priest, he remains full of sin. He must now live with this anger, which he cannot give to anyone else. He coasts languidly along the beach. He does not care to hurry. He will not sleep tonight.

PEARCE

Hobart-town, July 1824 A.D.

The fluid echo of water in Alexander's cell prises him from his half sleep. Day clings to the rising sun, and the sounds of the living world grow in subtle mingling above. Alexander feels his smooth jaw. Conolly will be pleased that he shaved.

The drip is eclipsed by footsteps. Two pairs clap with one another. No words of eternity are on Conolly's lips when he arrives. How did you sleep? he asks. Alexander is glad to hear it.

John Bisdee gives them some time alone. For the last time, the priest enters with his habitual black bible and long sheets of paper filled with words. Conolly has never brought a script before. Conolly looks at Alexander then down to his notes. Your confession, he explains. These words are for the crowd. I am going to speak for you, Alexander, if you don't mind. I thought you might like that.

Alexander does not care. He had no intention of speaking anyway. Nonetheless, he asks out of interest: What do you intend to say on my behalf?

That you are penitent. 'Tis all Governor Arthur wants to hear.

Of course, thinks Alexander. The governor.

These are the words of your own confession anyway, Conolly glosses. You will be heard, in the end, even if I speak for you.

The end. They are words like a breath in the sawpit of Alexander's soul which stir up that old unwillingness to go.

Conolly had called him a coward. He wonders if it is the weaker or stronger men who would kill themselves in the same positions. His heart may now be painted with lime and washed clean of nerve and feeling, but there is one sensation which remains; he is not choosing to die.

He thinks of all the miles he has crossed – every mouth told him he was the first to venture so far – all the terror he has endured. He has not been rewarded for it. But you killed and ate a man, he says to himself. You are not allowed to do that. So you must pay for it. It is as Conolly says: one cannot disagree with the bible. He only wishes it were easier, like in sleep. No sleep on the gallows. You have to face this, Alexander, a voice says to him.

Conolly takes the eucharist once more and prays with Alexander. They do the confession again, although Alexander thinks that if he sinned while he was asleep then all humanity is damned.

They take the flesh of Christ, and the blood. It tastes nothing like flesh and blood, Alexander thinks. He wonders if his smile is a sin. Conolly's glance is querulous.

Despite these thoughts he trusts Conolly. Alexander takes the names of David and Virgil and tosses them aside like dross: there should be a church in Phillip Conolly's name.

Are you ready to eat? Conolly asks. Alexander's stomach gives its own answer. In the draughty bastion upstairs Alexander is seated and fed. He does not touch the pork.

While he waits with Conolly, he thinks of every road he has ever worked on. His mind drifts to each morsel of rock he has ever crushed. He built bridges. He formed roads. He scoured forests. What was it for?

He sits at the table looking at Conolly, who is ever expectant and eager to elicit scripture, and wonders who is truly to blame. He remembers Conolly telling him his salvation begins where his excuses end. Yes, his state is his fault, but his fault is also his state.

The constables pass in and out, and the sober wall is smeared with changing sun. Watching the light transform, Alexander feels unfortunately hard and pale and hollow like driftwood.

Death or liberty. He glances at the blue marks on his forearm. He is stranded somewhere between the two − awake and sober, and unable to be rid of the film of anger which sticks to everything heaped upon him. He looks at Conolly and wonders if he has thrown away the brooch. Perhaps it hurts him as much as it hurts Alexander. He should have been rid of the ill omen years ago. But he looks at his arm, faded and blue and distinct. He would have carried this mark anyway. He is wrong to blame the brooch. His misses it and wishes its familiar grooves were inside his palm.

He feels now his smooth jaw and is conscious that Conolly has not commented on it. You'd best shave, Conolly had said. For whose benefit? The governor's? He imagines the swimming faces of the crowd below the gibbet. He remembers Scattergood's run and the chain-gang. Can he believe that he was made to work as a consequence of his crimes?

Alexander feels himself slipping into the verges of awful doubt. The complaints of so many convicts of his past come to him: We are prisoners of an unknown war. A thousand voices proclaim. If it is true, then Alexander's crimes were a consequence of the work he was enslaved to do – that he had thieved as a young man was irrelevant.

They did not care for his hunger, those masters who built the colonies, those who profited from them. Many men had been condemned to death in the old country and had their sentences revoked for transportation. That was not mercy. Only when they cannot be milked any more for their labour are these same men hanged – that is proof if nothing else.

Will you spend forever here? Alexander asks the priest quietly after some time. He is seeking the feeling of a thought to destroy the dark proud doubts that have risen in his quiet, drifting mind, dark proud doubts which tell him he is innocent.

Yes. I'll die here like you.

That is a cynical thought, now.

Cynicism is a form of optimism, says Conolly. I'm hopeful

that not everything is as it seems.

At present the door to the yard opens and the sheriff strides in with constables. But Alexander is not looking at them. He is looking at Conolly and he is smiling.

Are you ready, Reverend Conolly? the sheriff asks. Conolly nods. He touches Alexander on the arm. Together they rise and pass into the yard.

The scaffold looms ahead. The pallor of the sky is boxed inside its frame. Voices gather and mix and pull apart in the gulf beyond the stone wall. Far beyond them, where the Derwent folds hands with the estuary of the sea, Alexander comprehends calling gulls. It feels like a long moment and a long walk but it could be covered with the toss of a stone. Alexander comes to the top of the gallows stair and sees the faceless hangman. He looks upon the closed edges of the square platform which will carry him away like a falling sail. He does not look at the crowd who surely gawk below. He looks instead through the air to the court house of dun sandstone, then to St David's church. He turns his neck in the direction of the blackwoods which grow over the graveyard where Lieutenant Cuthbertson has been reinterred. He is appeased and depressed at once that he will not be buried in that place. That is a place where gentlemen are buried. He tries to remove his mind from these places. He fills his eyes instead with the sea from whence he had come. He does not look at the crowd but deep in his heart he hopes they will sing for him.

The moment drags and nobody sings. But Alexander can go

without singing – as Conolly brushes past him he sees a white brooch pinned to his breast. Conolly raises his notes and speaks to the crowd.

Here is a man, Conolly begins by murmuring. He goes on in audible English speech: Alexander Pearce, standing on the awful entrance into eternity on which he is placed, much desires to make the most public acknowledgement of his guilt in order to humble himself, as much as he may, in the sight of God and man.

I see many of you before me chequered in black and yellow. I see many of you in shackles. Do not think these instruments of the law to be unnecessary things. Though you are in bonds, it is for your salvation that you are so bound.

Alexander cannot be sure if Conolly means to lie, and if he does, who he will confess to for it.

The unfortunate Pearce is more willing to die than to live. Today we see the laws of Moses fulfilled—that is our vindication—but I ask, for the sake of all our souls, that you here today offer up your prayers for this man so condemned.

There is a clamour of groans and bovine lowing in the crowd. Conolly raises his voice above them: And beg of the Almighty to have mercy upon him ... as we would hope the Almighty grants mercy unto us all.

Alexander wonders how many will pray for him. The noose is placed over his neck. The knot rests upon his shoulder. He does not think many will.

He does not have time to reflect any more on Conolly's

words. Conolly turns to face him. He gives a tortured smile to Alexander before Alexander's vision is wilted by a falling white hood.

He feels his breath upon his face. Conolly's black vestments, the dun clouds, the purple mountains – it is all diminished into swaying shadows. What remains is the smell of the sea and his own dormant, paranoid sweat. Alexander hears Conolly's voice through the calico hood: Pearce, can you hear me?

Yes.

Conolly begins to pray in Irish: Father God, I admit this man into your keeping …

All Alexander can see now is snow. Then he loses the feeling of Conolly's hands. He closes his eyes and sees darkness. He opens them again and sees light. In the flashes are disclosed Macquarie Harbour's burgundy water, the bright bile of deep forests, the buds of Monaghan sheep; he feels his mother's wet kiss on his forehead. Drawing these colours to one side, his eyes rest on a thin stroke of black in the pale blur of his hood. Conolly. The head of the shape shifts and bends in a definite nod. Alexander holds back his breath. He wonders if the journey will be long.

EPILOGUE

Hobart-town, 1834 A.D.

It has become something of a tradition for Phillip to share a picnic with Sophia every Sunday after service. She allows him to pick the location, as it is she who provides the rug, the food and the wine. Some Sundays he uses his imagination, but most of the time he picks the old cemetery.

Sophia does not question his choice – she must think him a gothic old man now. Phillip does not tell Sophia this, but he picks the old cemetery, not because Mary Ann is buried there, but because it is the one spot he believes has changed the least in 14 years. He does not think this is a good thing or a bad thing – it is just a place – but it feels different to everywhere else. From the high bank of tufted grass Phillip can see the broad throat of the southern ocean between two points of fading land. At his back Mount Wellington is in snow. The gulls debate the naval bells. The flowers are joining the spring.

There are large ships pushing away from old Hunter Island. It was once the gateway to Hobart-town. Now its little channel has been swallowed up by reclaimed land. Burly men bear bales of wool upon their shoulders. Tight uniforms carry discreet conversations with harbourmasters. Foaming sheets of the sea test their reach upon the sand.

Phillip peers above the seawracked offing towards a crooked peninsula which stretches east. There is a faint blue wrinkle of land in the distance. Phillip believes he can see the hump of a tor lately renamed Mount Arthur, standing above the port that he cannot see.

The governor could have called Port Arthur something a little more inspiring, Phillip says out loud, rather than pissing on it like a dog. Why must governors give their names to everything?

Sophia does not bite at the joke, being distracted by her son, so Phillip trails off: Impotency, maybe.

What are you grumbling about? she speaks at last, a six year old in her arms.

Phillip sits on Sophia's rug surrounded by Sophia's earthenware, Sophia's cushions and Sophia's refreshments. He is so poor he does not know why she continues to invite him to picnics, but he is glad that she does.

Will you look at the bees here, Jack, Phillip hoists his voice up to a high note.

Sophia draws her son's attention elsewhere, bobbing him in her arms. Look at those very big ships, my darling. Little Jack is more interested in the tall ships than the bees.

The last ships of Macquarie Harbour have called in Sullivan's Cove. Now they are departing. One of the vast vessels beats its vaulting wings, followed by the others.

I think it's beautiful to watch ships depart at a distance, Sophia says.

Beautiful? They are prison ships. Phillip is dour as he speaks.

I think for something to be beautiful it ought to have a little sadness in it. Sophia looks closely in her sons eyes.

Yes, but not this.

It can be beautiful and sad at once.

Spoken from a high luxurious balcony, that phrase. Phillip's own bitter note arrests him. He stands from the rug and takes Sophia's hand, rubbing it to apologise for his crudeness. My age, he excuses. His bitterness must be regular, for Sophia seems accustomed to it.

What's the matter with you? she asks.

Phillip sighs. He looks up the hill to where the grey box of St Virgil's shivers in the wind. It is a building despised by more than half the gentry of Hobart-town who claim Phillip lives off public funds. That is part of the matter, thinks Phillip. For all that he has done for the colony; they will not even concede to him a pillow for his head. Sophia is usually a remedy for these sores, but to ask him the matter sets rogue thoughts in a sea he's been trying to settle.

I'm getting old, Sophia. Too old for pastoral work.

You're not a pastoralist.

I work with sheep, don't I? 'Tis labour to be a shepherd. No wonder Christ only worked for three years.

That's not very funny.

Phillip shrugs. Again, put it down to my age. How are things in town?

Busy. There is much talk about the new penal settlement at Port Arthur. Sophia looks again upon the prison ships retiring from the bay.

What is there to talk about? Phillip is aware of his melancholy.

It is the new system. The model prison.

New, is all Phillip can say. The word hangs in the air like a whispered protest in the gust of a locomotive. The government closed Sarah Island 12 months ago. At last rebellion, disease and murder broke her.

That was the official story. Phillip knows better. After the last commandant resigned, a shipbuilder named David Hoy had arrived in the harbour. He had travelled there in search of the fabled timber which does not rot.

Although the officials speak of the last years of Macquarie Harbour as though they were as wretched as its first, when Lieutenant Cuthbertson had charge, the truth disagrees. Sarah Island became a productive shipyard under David Hoy.

But Governor Arthur caught wind, and Phillip wonders still if the man has a sadistic knot in his character which will not let him sleep unless he knows the lowest rung of society is being stepped upon by the heel. Sarah Island was to be a place of punishment, insisted the governor, not a place where labour is rewarded – so it was closed down.

New.

Sophia and Phillip sit together on the rug. Sophia says, The mind of the reformer is changing. The prison system in England bears good results. The men and women are made penitent through reflection and hard labour, not through being brutalised.

The notion of new sentiments revives a conversation Phillip had with Bobby Knopwood years before. They had spoken of old pains, as though crossing half the world would leave such things behind.

He tries to warm his eyes for Sophia. He says, Ventriloquism. I believe every word you just said has come from your husband, Thomas.

Sophia's face wrinkles. Thomas Walker is a man of high ideas, if he is a prisoner, and unlike his new wife, he can read. Phillip speaks often with Thomas on these matters.

Phillip watches six-year-old Jack chase a spinning top. He recalls the day Sophia came to him asking for a place to stay away from Hellings; she had fallen pregnant to another man. Hellings would have killed her for it.

It should not be that sin opens the door to freedom, yet, were it not for Thomas Walker and the night Jack was conceived, Phillip thinks Sophia might never have left Hellings. Now she lives with her husband at Green Ponds. She has employment and a son, and for eight years Sophia has held a certificate of freedom, her seven-year sentence complete.

Please tell Thomas he is a fool if he believes that the mind of the reformer is changing, Phillip picks up, warning himself even as he speaks to water the bitterness down – he would rue missing even one picnic if Sophia decided he was crabby company.

Phillip advances an explanation: Macquarie Harbour has stained the face of the colony through years of cannibalism and carnage. And now the governor believes he can redress those years of torture and turn back the wicked clock.

Don't you believe, Phillip, these nightmares were brought on by the calibre of men interned there? Sophia asks. How quickly a freed person forgets their former bonds, thinks Phillip.

Calibre of men, certainly; you did not meet the men that *ran* it. I adored Sorell as many people did, but now in looking back I see with much regret the wrong that was done.

You must be relieved, then, that they have given up the lash for quiet reformation.

O Sophia. Do not believe any less damage is done to a creature when you punish its mind instead of its body. The days of breaking men at Macquarie Harbour may now be history— and history we would sooner forget—but I believe the demented outcomes of breaking minds lay only in front of us now.

Phillip feels the pang of an unwanted trail of memories. Eyes as green as his memory of Ireland arrive uninvited. He has not seen Johanna or her children since she opened a bawdy house on the far side of town. He can never speak to her again, although every day he waits for her to walk up the hill to St

Virgil's, as Sophia did six years ago.

How can you be sure? Sophia is intent on knowing.

Because I have seen what both the torture of body and torture of mind can drive a man to do. Back then, I wouldn't have thought that long hours of solitude would break a man as much as the whip.

Are you speaking of Pearce?

He need not be the only one, but yes, I speak of Alexander Pearce. Do you know what he endured?

I know what he did.

Easier to see the monster, Phillip throws aside. The love of condemnation in this colony has long been its peril. I scorn, but I am old and grumpy. Phillip's hands fall idly to his knees. Sophia gives one hand a squeeze.

Do you think he was in any way redeemable?

That is for God to answer. All I know is that while the lash drove him into the wilderness, it was his time in the wilderness that sent him to hell. Did you know we were both from county Monaghan?

And look at you, Sophia reaches for a point.

Phillip feels tears in his eyes: Aye. Look at me. And look at Cuthbertson. He is presently aware that they sit in a graveyard. He recalls the afternoon when surgeon James Scott took the body of Pearce away to be dissected. Even today, Phillip thinks, there are those who believe the shape of a skull can reveal something of a person's nature. *Study his past,* Phillip thought then. *That will tell you more about his mind than the shape of his bones.*

Do not sing my praise, Sophia. I chose to come here. That was a freedom given to me. Yes, we were born in the same county … but born in the same world? He lets the question hang.

Do you think God decides our destiny?

I think we choose. But a common mouse born in the hole of an aristocrat's larder will eat better than a mouse born in the barn. To the matter of those choices … yes, we choose. It is a matter of what we are given to choose from.

The bell tolls high noon.

Pa will be at the end of his work, Sophia calls out to her son. Come Jack, we're going.

Phillip looks to the belltower of St David's, then to the collapsed grounds of the old gaol where he used to stand and usher men into eternity. There is a new penitentiary on the other side of town, just as there is the new harbour prison away to the south – both bring forth new branches of prisoners, like the green and thorny shoots of last winter's dormant blackberry stock. *How the old world fades*, Phillip thinks.

Sophia picks up her son. Phillip regards the boy's bright face. He retires his bitterness on the hope that a fairer future rests in the unsullied eyes of Sophia's son.

The bell tolls again.

Shall we go? Sophia asks, tugging on Phillip's hand.

Yes, let's go. He takes a final survey of the snows beneath Mount Wellington, and together they pass into Hobart-town.

ACKNOWLEDGEMENTS

Much changes in four years.

In that time, the writing of this novel has been touched by many hands – conscious and unaware. I would like to thank them briefly here.

Firstly, to my brother, William, who followed me to the sodden bogs of Kelly's Basin, chasing ghosts. My love for Tasmania is so wide that I am grateful to share it with you.

Secondly, my dear friends Andrew and Laura, who stuck the manuscript to the wall and were constant in their belief that the story was worth telling – even when I was not so sure. I promise it is finished now.

I owe both a special thanks – Andrew, for assisting in the typesetting of this novel, and Laura, for reading its earliest incarnations; your advice made the difference.

My parents have ensured that I have not had to starve for my art – for that I am humble and grateful.

Although I have not met Paul Collins (*Hell's Gates*) or James Boyce (*Van Diemen's Land*), nor was I fortunate enough to meet the late Richard Davey, I owe a debt to their research, which dug the foundations of this novel. I feel compelled to credit Davey's Round Earth Theatre Company, which produces Australia's longest consecutive-running production, *The Ship That Never Was*. It was the captivating performance of one of their actors, David Pidd, which first introduced me to Sarah Island. It has stayed with me since. David is a fine actor who has even influenced some of the characters in this novel, although he does not know it.

I also owe thanks to Brendan Lennard, former historian for the city of Hobart, who furnished me with the following photograph.

Reverend S. C. Brammall, 1926. St David's Park, Hobart. TAHO, series NS2822.

At that time, I was searching for the grave of Lieutenant John Cuthbertson. Brendan advised me that the old burial ground was cleared for a recreation park in 1926. Most of the old headstones were destroyed. Only a few major monuments remained.

Many broken headstones lined the edge of the park until the 1970s when their crumbling remnants were removed permanently. Cuthbertson's memorial had long since disappeared.

Brendan was gracious enough to provide me with the inscription from the lieutenant's missing headstone, salvaged from the record books. In the absence of heirlooms, moments of revelation like this – as with performances like David's – have given the breath of life to this novel.

When it existed, the inscription on Cuthbertson's headstone closed with: This stone records his meritorious services and his unhappy fate.

I know this is only a transcription, Brendan said, but in the absence of the monument, it's all we have.

I hope this novel stands as a long inscription to a moment in time that must not be forgotten. Brammall's photograph lends the words of Shakespeare to this purpose: Imperial Caesar, dead and turned to clay, might stop a hole to keep the wind away.

The monuments of our past all wear away, until they are the dust which dirties our carpet – or, more optimistic, the mortar that holds our houses together. In Phillip Conolly's words: How the old world fades …

Or doesn't fade at all. In this case, I hope it does not fade so quick that we cannot learn from it.

R. B. R. Verhagen